YOUЯ
NAME
HEЯE
PAINT BOMB
BIG DEAL©96

THE GRINNING GARGOYLE SPILLS THE BEANS

And Other Yarns of Baja California

by

J. P. "Jimmy" Smith, Jr.

ISBN 0-9644066-1-6
Printed in the United States of America
Published by Baja Source, Inc.
1945 Dehesq Rd. El Cajon, CA 92019
Phone/fax (619) 442-7061

Por Doña Guadalupe del Socorro Romero Lopez de Smith...

Mí Compañera

"Jim Smith could start a
conversation
with a dead dog."

-Mark Willis

CONTENTS

CONTENTS

WHAT IS BAJA TO ME...? J.P. SMITH JR.!

- Illustrator's forward-

That's not a by-line. I remember one evening in 1959, during my college days, while hanging out at the Rosarita Beach Hotel with Jack Palance (actually I just had one drink with him, big tall guy), this was the night before the f*ederales* busted the place for gambling and the Kingston Trio made the "Tijuana Jail" an infamous place in song and history. I walked out to the main (only) road and down the bridge and looked south. I thought to myself, "One day I have to go down that road."

About five years later, I read a story in the LA Times Sunday supplement, *West Magazine,* about the Baja California Peninsula and a trip in an old Studebaker truck by Charles Portis, who later authored *True Grit*. In this story a strange gringo named Jimmy Smith was mentioned as having a dispute with Frank Fisher, a WWI German immigrant and well known Baja fixture. I made a mental note, because the dispute was in the picturesque town of San Ignacio. I had read an article in *Matador Magazine* about this quaint little town, and intended to go there someday and get some sand in my shoes. About this same time, 1965, I made my first trip to Mexico City in my beater 1953 bus, and generally loved Mexico enough to seriously start learning the palaver.

Move forward in time about two years and voila! Jimmy Smith's and my path finally crossed in Roger Smith's backyard (VW Peppertree Automotive) in Costa Mesa California.

We hit it off immediately and soon we were flying around southern California in a little Cessna 172 airplane. After the flight, Jimmy sided me over to a flight instructor, paid five bucks, and after a half-hour flight I found myself in possession of a logbook and an altered status in life; that of a new student pilot. That's another story, but I must say it was Jim that helped me get off the stick and realize my lifelong love of aviation. Jim first showed me how to cross the border in a light aircraft, something I could have read from a book I guess, but that's not how it worked out. He introduced me to the real Baja, and many of his wonderful Californio amigos along the way.

We flew to San Ignacio with my wife Velia, son Travis, and Jim's daughter Sally, and I definitely got sand in my shoes. I met Guadalupe, Jim's future wife, there that trip. I went back many times both racing and in my airplane: with Jim, for Jim, and twenty years later, *looking* for Jim (presumed "lost" in a storm in the Baja Raja). We raced the Baja 1000 together in 1967. We slept in the desert without sleeping bags in November near Punta Prieta. We discovered that gasoline and STP on cholla cactus works fairly well in lieu of more sensible sleeping arrangements. My introduction to Baja and flying were results of this old cowboy from west Texas. And there was something about life I learned from Jim too.

You know it could have been the Rub-al Kali in Saudi Arabia, the Tarin Basin in Asia, the Khyber pass in Afganistan, or Agri province in eastern Turkey (which is a lot like Mexico, by the way). It wouldn't have mattered where in the world we drove or flew, and it isn't really about Baja so much for me, although Baja is a fantastic place, a place I love and have come to know fairly intimately - Baja California is Jim Smith to me.

He *is* the Grinning Gargoyle of Baja California after all, isn't he? I'm proud to say he's my friend. Heck, you ask if I know J.P. Smith, Jr? Yeah, we had lunch together once.

Dave Deal
(The one who scribbled the illustrations in this here book.)

AUTHOR'S PREFACE

The working title of this dubious document was BX (beta chi) under the assumption that it (the book) was too classy to be termed as pure bullshit and therefore became BOVINE EXCREMENT or simply BX. The floppy disks housing the manuscript are numbered BX 1, BX 2, BX 3 and so on.

My motivation for writing this book conforms to an observation made by Colonel Harvey K. Greenlaw in about 1954 wherein he stated, "Everyone who travels down the Baja California Peninsula seems to be overwhelmed by a desire to write a book about the goddamn place. I suppose you will do the same." I promised the Colonel that no book was forthcoming until I was qualified to write one. While I'm still unqualified, my seventy-fourth year is here so it's now or never. Forgive me Colonel! Further motivation was supplied by audiences in hotel bars here on the East Cape when they asked, "Jim, when are you going to write a book?"

Fred Hoctor implies that these stories were polished while I was shilling beers in those hotel barrooms. This may very well be true.

Some observations herein may be construed by certain readers as being a little rough on Mexican culture and politics. As a Mexican and the head of a vast Mexican family, I submit that I am endowed with this prerogative. As for derogatory observations concerning the gringos, somebody has to do it!

Many debts have been incurred in the preparation of this manuscript. I should like to acknowledge a few: Bob & Chacha Van Wormer, Cathi Brown (she can spell) Les Brown (some of my best punch lines) Sally Lask (sure pop, you can do it,) my wife, Lupe (I don't know what you're doing in that trailer, but it keeps you out of barrooms,) my granddaughter Tehroma Lask, Leon & Cathi Martin who kept my word processor running, Joann Hyslop (if a story pissed her off, I knew it was a keeper,) darlin' Josephine Quinn (she wasn't all that impressed,) Bob and Mary Bowmen (my cheerleaders,)

Joanne & Ed Altman who supplied some good research, Abel & Hilda Aguilar, Hercilia Ceseña, Mark Willis, Duane & Lisa (Mullet) Culberson, Ken McDowell (he smuggled me cigarettes,) Lee & Arleen Bray, Manuel (Chacho) Meza, Mike Werner, Dr. Alan Dray, Richard Weaver (for assistance with publication), Gustavo (Tavo) Villacencio, Anna Maria Hamlin, Fredrico (Liko) Verdugo, Sheila Barnett, Dick Maugg, Earl Maynard, Teri & Mike O'Dell, Rebecca (Bekita) Leree de Castro, Kaki Bassi, Cliff Ferguson, Marsh McCoy, Steve Chism (who wore out a car helping with research,) Gene Morford, Ray Strait, Mike & Nancy Briening, Mike & Donna Russel, Rafael Martinez, Paul (Tio Pablo) Gilbert, Paul and Olida Thompson and many others.

Last but not least kudos go to my bearded buddy Dave Deal and his lovely wife, Vicki (she has no beard,) who have tolerated my BX for around thirty years and were my chief source of encouragement when it looked like I would never finish.

Mike Briening swears this is true. He called Dave's house and Vicki answered.

"Where's Dave?"

"Oh, he's bullshittin' down Baja with Jim Smith," she replied.

"Bullshittin' Down Baja" was seriously considered as a title for this work!

Ginger McMahan Potter contributed her merciless blue pencil. When it was a bad story or didn't fit, she slashed with less compassion than Genghis Kahn, when it was right, she made me feel taller than Magic Johnson, while husband, Chuck, tolerantly laid back and grinned at our proceedings. God bless him! Our darlin' Kate Lansdown took up editorial duties at Baja Source after Ginger's death and finished the job.

Finally, *muchas gracias* to Gene Kira (the pro) who made many constructive suggestions on the manuscript.

Jim Smith
Los Barriles, B.C.S.

HOW I MET THE FAMOUS AUTHOR AND...LIKETHAT...

For some thirty years now Hercilia Briseña's pharmacy on Calle Morales in San Ignacio has been utilized as a domino parlor, a meeting place for lovers, a general social emporium, a political headquarters and a cat breeding farm. Long and lazy afternoons were expended there as Hercilia taught me the rudiments of *dominado*, *decimales* and the Spanish language.

As a result, my wife, Guadalupe swears my first intelligible sentence in Spanish was "*Que bonitas nalgas tiene usted*" ("What a lovely posterior you have"). Hercilia spent an inordinate amount of time spoon feeding me this statement. Some thirty years have not altered my opinion of its validity.

My mornings, in those days, were consumed by bashing my skull against an old Underwood typewriter in an effort to create the great American novel set in Baja California. While as a novel the manuscript was a total failure, there was a certain vein of local history, geography and folklore that was well researched.

Enter Famous Author. His gimmick was a shyster lawyer who through devious means soundly thumped a demented police detective in about two hundred pages with nauseating regularity. You can't argue with success. He sold millions of paperback books and a long running television series. He also wrote several very bad hardbound volumes, which he represented as the gospel truth on Baja California.

First contact was established when an afternoon domino session was brought to a screeching focus by his need for some photos of Hercilia for publication as she was a very pretty girl and is presently a lovely matron. I was impressed.

Since Casa Leree was the only hotel in town and dinner was served at a single table and at a fixed hour, Famous Author and I were messmates that evening. He viewed some of my manuscripts, stated they had some possibility and condescended to show them to his publisher.

He subsequently reported that while as a novelist I was a total failure, I did have certain ability as a researcher and he offered a minuscule subsidy should I continue research with the understanding that the resulting data was his property. While below minimum wage in the land of the big PX, this subsidy would put me an equal pay scale with the local schoolmaster. I eagerly set out to unearth scholarly information for Mr. Famous Author to "discover".

As this arrangement matured, it became apparent that by using FA's name I could con free lodging from sport fishing resorts and numerous other amenities (e.g., a major motorcycle manufacturer supplied dirt bikes for my wanderings anticipating mention or photos in one of FA's forthcoming books).

I soon learned that FA had 2 addictions: (1) "I was there first" (2) arrowheads.

"I was the first white man to view the painted caves of Sierra San Francisco"... Fact: These caves were on Leree land. Francisco Leree was a French mining engineer and FA had a German blacksmith direct his helicopter to the site. His first knowledge of the site was supplied by his gringo research assistant (yours truly). I wonder how his devious attorney, Mr. Bricklayer would handle that one.

On arrowheads he was a fanatic. He spent literally months scratching around in abandoned Indian caves and kitchen middens in this quest. It became my stock in trade to see that he never failed.

Hipolito Arce, a *ranchero* from the sierra, loved tequila. Hipolito seemed to have a never-ending supply of Cochimí points, which could be bartered for tequila. If he found these arrowheads, he didn't accomplish much ranching so I assumed that he manufactured them. This secret died with Hipolito.

The OO affixed to the front of my decrepit Underwood were returning my baleful stare when the below listed telegraphic message intruded:

ARRIVING LAS CASITAS MULEGÉ
THURSDAY STOP
EXPECT U THERE STOP
FA

Wednesday afternoon found me present and accounted for in Fred and Cuca Woodworth's Las Casitas Bar. Fred, Bill Lloyd and I had consumed an admirable quantity of a rum concoction called *sepillo* when the subject of arrowheads came up. I displayed my supply and revealed my evil intent involving a plan to salt a cave or two assuring FA's usual success. After a proper interval of admiration, Fred disappeared and returned with a small bottle of white paint, a three hair lettering brush and a magnifying glass. Fred had been a commercial artist in the real world and did a bang up job of printing MADE IN JAPAN in minute letters on a goodly number of prime specimens.

While the glow of the *sepillos* was still on us, we set off on a cave salting expedition. It seemed we were doing a great job at the time, but we must have been a bit overly enthusiastic as we later observed about half a pint of arrowheads had been utilized in a small cave.

FA's *modus operandi* entailed utilization of small Mexican boys as guides as they were naïve, honest, enthusiastic and worked cheap. We located a couple of *chamacos*, briefed and bribed them, and returned to the business at hand, to wit: *SEPILLOS*. We retired rather late that night.

The burden of a record-breaking hangover was somewhat compounded around noontime the following day by the news of FA's arrival. He had arrived complete with entourage in the early morning and been captured by my co-conspiring *chamacos*. They were off in the caves hunting arrowheads.

Haggard and happy, FA put in an appearance at Las Casitas around 6:00 P.M. and announced, "I was the first white man to view Baja California's largest arrowhead sediment." He also revealed that he had stopped by the telegraph office to summon an emanate archeologist to confirm this astounding find. I responded in kind by ordering another bloody Mary.

Dr. X flew in from U.B.X. the next afternoon and went directly to Casitas Hotel where the find was laid out atop the bar on green felt. "My God, FA," he said, "these are lovely, some of the finest specimens of

Cochimí arrowheads I have seen … oops; what have we here?" He produced a magnifying glass from somewhere and scanned Fred's handiwork while he ground his teeth.

To dispense with certain sordid details, let's say that I was unemployed, packed and enroute to San Ignacio before dinner.

FA continued to create bad books and magazine articles on Baja California. In these I appeared as a craven coward, a cad, a pirate, an uncouth expatriate and a trespasser in his private Baja California. He never mentioned me by name but applied the pseudonym; "THE GRINNING GARGOYLE OF SAN IGNACIO."

Several years subsequent to these events, Dave Deal designed and presented me with a thousand calling cards. Thus, I became *The Grinning Gargoyle of Baja California.* Dave stated that a man of my stature should not be confined to villainy in one small pueblo.

ESMERALDA DODGE

In 1957, through a process that has escaped my memory, I met and immediately loved a rather nondescript appearing dowager, Miss Esmeralda Dodge, familiarly "Ezzy." Ezzy, of noble pedigree but doubtful reputation, had a most interesting history. She had been seen in the company of various soldiers in World War II. She labored on a farm in the Imperial Valley of California. She worked on a pipeline in the Mojave Desert and prospected for uranium in Utah. Ezzy had been around. She boasted of ancestors who had accompanied Dr. Roy Chapman Andrews in his Gobi Desert exploration. We all know the family, the famous Dodge Brothers of Detroit, lately associated with the Chrysler Company there.

Ezzy has many aliases, categorically she was first known as a "Jeep". Her cute little cousin, the Willys, stole that name from her (the Willys was called "Peep" in those days) so she became the command car. As she gained fame, the army saw fit to give her the unglamorous title of four by four. Ezzy's body was changed and she became a bomb carrier. An ambulance ensued. A later modification was the weapons carrier, much cherished by combat troops. After the war, she became the brute Power Wagon. The people of Baja California called her "Comando." I called her Ezzy, for she was truly female. When mistreated, she broke a spring. When not given attention, she burned out ignition points. When caressed, she rewarded me with perfect performance.

Ezzy found Baja California much to her liking. Her huge balloon tires floated nicely over the rocks of the Camino Real. The mushy sands of Laguna Salada, while they would mire her chromed cousins, caused her to purr with delight. The Aguajito Hill, a rise of seventeen-hundred feet in two miles, gave her transmission an opportunity to whine of persecution and her proud old engine to bellow with rage.

When I obtained Ezzy, she had been in Utah, hunting U-235s with some pipe dreaming shoe clerks. They found nothing. If their knowledge of prospecting was as small as their knowledge of care and feeding of fine trucks, it is a small wonder. A new engine, a new front axle, and an infinite amount of tender loving care soon had her road worthy and eager.

Experience taught Ezzy and me many things. We always carried at least seventy gallons of gasoline at the initiation of our treks. Many spare parts were carried as insurance. Extra springs, ignition points, a starter, a generator, spare transmission gears and bearings, a new carburetor, and a fan belt would represent only a small part of the inventory. Among my tools, I considered a small oxy-acetylene welding apparatus an essential item.

Custom demands that the traveler in Baja California assist all who are in trouble. I seldom needed the spare parts and equipment but frequently found them invaluable in assisting other travelers.

Ezzy and I once found a fellow with a broken frame on his boat trailer between Puertocitos and the Bay of San Luis Gonzaga. I did not have a welder at that time. It was necessary to drill holes in the trailer frame to admit bolts to fasten the frame together with a fishplate. We had no drill either. Smith and Wesson supplied a rather novel solution. Armor piercing loads of a .357 revolver did a neat job indeed.

The gentleman with the broken trailer was Mr. F. Gordon Duff, one of the largest welding supply dealers in the Los Angeles area. He later gave me my oxy-acetylene welder with instructions that I would never again be on the peninsula without this piece of equipment. Many bridle bits, spurs and windmills were brazed or welded back together courtesy of Mr. Duff.

In the ensuing seven years, Ezzy and I spent many months on the Viscíano Desert; searching for the lost mission in the Sierra Santa Clara, hanging out with Tata (Grandpa) Murillo while he prospected on the Desierto Pintada. We watched the wildlife at the Ojo de Liebre waterhole and inspected the flotsam and jetsam on Playa Malarrimo (now commonly called Scavenger's Beach).

Occasionally we had company, but mostly it was Ezzy, books, an old Zenith Transoceanic radio and I. We kept our own pace that way and conformed to the old Mexican proverb:

"Mas vale solo que con mala compañía."
("Tis better to be alone than in bad company.")

Esmeralda Dodge became a permanent resident of San Ignacio in 1965. Oscar Fischer finally convinced me to sell the truck when I went to the East Cape to become involved in fishing resort management. She died there. I saw her carcass near the Hotel Posada San Ignacio last year.

THE HUECO

Lupe calls it my *hueco* (hole in the ground in which spiders and rabbits live, den, lair, nest). Actually it's an old Taveleze trailer that Uncle Tom Turpin left me when he died.

The whole village knows that Lupe gets meaner than a damned snake when the moon is full. Uncle Tom put it in his will that he wanted me to have a place to sleep when the moon gets round. He left me his trailer.

Lupe and Luli (our housekeeper) have pretty well banished me from the main house when I'm readin' and writin' and smokin' and generally bein' a dirty old man, so I have a hiding place where those damned fussy women can't come in and misplace or throw away everything each morning.

My *hueco* houses my father's Zane Grey collection, his Time/Life History of the West collection, my Louis Lamore collection, my John D. McDonald & James A. Michener stuff, The Complete Works of O'Henry, John Nichol's New Mexico Trilogy, Larry McMurtry's ravings, most of the Flying Magazines for the last fifteen years, some fifty books on Baja California and my old Apple IIc (now Macintosh) computer. My survival kit.

My *hueco* has the convenient facility of being portable. I can hook it up to my pick-up and be on my way in a matter of minutes. I think this fact has been a calming factor on my wife/mate during the last twenty years of full moons. She laid claim to the *hueco* until I translated Uncle Tom's will for her. The subject of the *hueco's* ownership hasn't come up lately.

ABUSES OF THE IDIOM

Spanglish, "as she is spake" here in the south end of Baja California, is a language unknown throughout the rest of the world. The tolerance and patience demonstrated by the native people is a singular courtesy, indeed.

Longtime associations between gringos and their Mexican friends and employees evolves into a system of communication which utilizes words and phrases that appear in neither English nor Spanish (my friend, Dick Maugg, adamantly believes that *perfectamundo is* found in all Spanish dictionaries). Both parties conclude that the word or phrase in question is of the other language and is frequently confused or misunderstood. Many long-time gringos fervently believe they have developed a fair grasp of the local idiom, when they are actually speaking a baby talk.

Place names suffer horribly! Depending on the individual real estate copywriter, the East Cape can lie anywhere between San José Del Cabo and La Paz. Cabo is understood among "hip gringos" to be the same place that the locals refer to as San Lucas. San Juanico is now Scorpion Bay and Punta Arena has become Lighthouse Point. Agua de la Costa is North Beach, while Rancho Buenas Aires is now the Goat Ranch. Ray Cannon baptized Puerto Cheleno and Cabaza de la Ballena as Shipwreck beach.

The peninsula suffers most. Drake called it New Albion. Cortez mixed Spanish and Latin (calidad = hot and fornax = furnace) and came up with California. As the northern areas of the pacific coast were conquered by the Franciscans, it became Antiqua California. At the end of the Mexican War, it was renamed Baja (Lower) California. When the first tourist penetrated after WW II, Baja California seemed too much effort and it became simply Baja. After the inaugural "off-road" race in 1967, GM decided to run a fleet of trucks down to La Paz for a publicity stunt. A Madison Avenue copywriter, who had not previously heard of the place, came up the nauseating caption "We Beat the Baja." The phrase "The Baja" grates on this author's nerves like someone scratching a blackboard with their fingernails.

Flora and fauna have not been ignored. Joseph W. Krutch when encountering the Cirio tree (*Idria columnaris*) assumed that since he did not have knowledge of that plant, no one else knew it existed. Pompously, he named it the boojum tree and called it the boojum in his book compounding the felony.

The dorado gets bruised a bit also. Those who wish to demonstrate their knowledge of Hawaiian lingo call it the mahi mahi. When young guests in hotels are informed they are eating dolphin, they immediately go into hysterics screaming, "Mommy, they're making me eat flipper!"

I thank you, sweet Jesus, that I will not be around in the year 2050 to decipher the language that I am certain will be called "Cabospeak!"

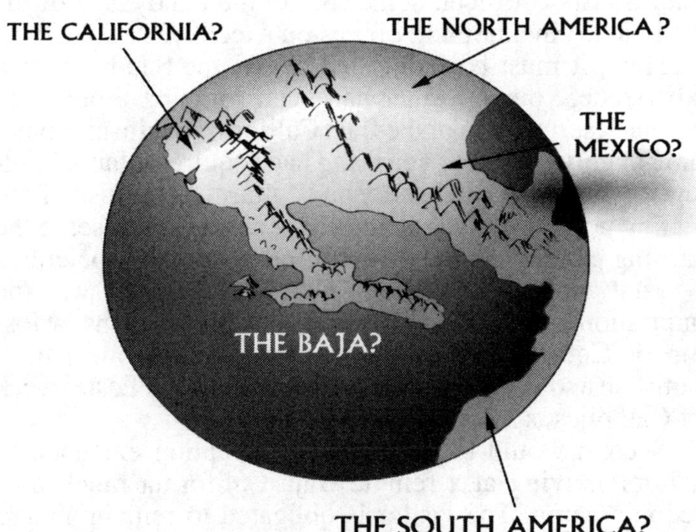

THE BEDOUINS OF BAJA

One of my greatest kicks is wandering throughout Baja California's backcountry in search of antiquities and associations with the old land grant families. Most of the people on the backcountry ranches can trace their lineage directly to the soldiers and craftsmen who served the Jesuit missionaries between 1697 and 1767. The most intriguing facets in relation to these highland people are how little their customs, language, and methods of ranch management have changed during the last three centuries.

Between 1977 and 1980 economic pressures forced this writer to become gainfully employed as chief transportation officer with AVCO/Dallah Corporation in the kingdom of Saudi Arabia. The company maintained all twenty-six military and civil airports in that country. One of the functions of my position was expediting the delivery of replacement motor vehicles to the various airports throughout the kingdom. Some of these airports were located in the outback of the Nafud and the vast Rub-al Kali Deserts. When the schedule permitted, deliveries to the most fascinating and remote historical sites were performed personally by the chief transport officer, somewhat to the annoyance of the candy asses in adjoining offices on executive row.

Here, it must be stated that before the Saudi Arabian experience, your informer had been romping around the remote desert sectors of the Baja California peninsula something over twenty-four years and had acquired a fair knowledge of the language, history and culture. At the risk of appearing pompous, I was somewhat qualified to observe the startling parallels in these two desert peninsular societies.

First and most apparent of these similarities was the unquestioning devotion to their individual religions - Moslem or Catholic. Strict adherence to religious ritual: Ramadan and Hadj for the Moslems or Lent and Easter week for Catholics is solemn and unvaried.

Second would be the identical reception extended to visitors arriving at a remote Baja California ranch or a Bedouin camp. The visitor is obligated to remain aboard his vehicle or mount (camel/horse) until an invitation to dismount is expressed and one is invited to enter the habitation (ranch house or Bedouin tent). Having entered, the visitor is immediately served coffee. During the coffee sipping ritual, the visitor is expected to relate an account of his journey.

The third similarity would be the attitude of the males of both cultures towards the fairer sex. The women in Arabic camps and highland ranches stay out of sight of male visitors until a long acquaintance is developed. It is considered a social blunder for a visiting male to inquire about women of the household in either culture. Polygamy is an accepted way of life in the Arabic society and while prohibited by the Catholic religion, is not unknown in some of the remote Baja California stations.

A non-compassionate, almost brutal treatment of animals in these two peoples is identical.

Newly married daughters-in-law are expected to live with the groom's family and are under the total dominance (and training) of the matriarch.

Methods of food preparation and table manners are very similar. Males eat while attended by the women who eat when the males have finished.

When remaining overnight, the visitor is offered the choice sleeping quarters in the habitation.

It was observed that Polaroid cameras had the same effect in the two societies. Years ago I wanted to get a look and shoot some photos in the famous old territorial prison in Mulegé. The guard on duty prohibited entry until he was presented a Polaroid photo of himself. He was so enthralled with this picture that he abandoned his post and left for home to show it to his family, leaving me to shoot all the pictures I wanted at my leisure. An identical occurrence was enacted while delivering a Dodge pick up to Sharoura Air Base on the Rub-al Kali Desert near the border of Yemen. Our convoy was halted by a patrol of the dreaded Damam Bedouin tribe. Things were a bit sticky until a snapshot from the trusty old Polaroid afforded us a passport and we continued our journey.

How did these parallels in the two cultures develop? Some say the moors passed it along from the Spaniards who had been dominant for eight hundred years. Others say these customs were inherited from the Indians. I don't know. Do you?

BOB DILL'S SHANGRI-LA

Canyon de la Zorra is a small mountain *rancharia* on the southern side of Sierra de la Laguna down behind the East Cape. Dr. Bobby Dill, a marine geologist of some note, became fascinated with the settlement several years ago because of the longevity of its inhabitants. Dill was interviewing a rather sturdy individual who alleged that he was ninety-six years old. When Dill expressed some doubt of this claim, the *anciano* summoned his mother from the kitchen to confirm its validity.

Don Luciano, a lifetime resident of Canyon de la Zorra, had never consulted a doctor in his life and the local physician in Santiago was somewhat taken aback when the Don appeared at his *consultorio* one morning.

"Doctor, I present myself for a revision," Don Luciano announced.

"Is there something in particular that ails you?" asked the medic.

"No, I wish to be assured that I am in good health as I am contemplating marriage."

The doctor was checking the old man's blood pressure when he mused, "How old are you, Don Luciano?"

"Seventy-three."

"And the bride?"

"Nineteen."

The doctor completed his examination and after a thoughtful moment said, "Don Luciano, for a man of seventy-three years, you are in remarkable health. However, if you are marrying a nineteen year old bride, I suggest that perhaps you should consider taking in a boarder."

"Very well, Doctor, your advice is well received and will be heeded," said Don Luciano as he took his leave.

Several months later, the doctor was once again amazed when Don Luciano appeared in his *consultorio*.

"Welcome, Don Luciano. How are you?"

"Fine, Doctor, fine."

"And the wife, Don Luciano?"

“Well, it’s about her that we come. We believe she is pregnant.”

“Marvelous, Don Luciano, and the boarder?”

“The boarder is here also as we think she is likewise pregnant.”

BUENA VISTA'S VOLUNTEER

FIRE DEPARTMENT

San José de Buena Vista acquired a slightly obsolete International Harvester fire pump through the auspices of the Sister Cities Program several years ago. It still flies the Victorville, California logo. Victorville Firemen were imported to train Fito Silva as engineer, fire chief and maintenance mechanic for this emergency vehicle.

Clinical analysis of Fito's personality can be boiled down to a single word - **MACHO**! All mechanical devices, in Fito's concept, must be operated at maximum volume whether they are automobiles, ghetto blasters, boats, motorcycles, or sirens. His daily equipment inspection includes a ten-minute serenade with the siren. Since the fire station is located adjacent to the only public telephone booth in the pueblo, communication ceases until Fito's inspection is complete. Fito is very proud of his post. Any movement of the fire vehicle is performed with all emergency equipment operating, even when the mission entails nothing more than a trip to top off the tank with water or to purchase gasoline. Four or five twelve-year-old urchins who always don the available fire helmets for the occasion usually accompany him.

Buena Vista's formidable fire department has logged only one fire call as this is written. It is reported that the spinster Gonzales sisters decided to burn some trash on a calm, spring evening and that a sudden windstorm started to spread the blaze. The Gonzales sisters live at the north limits of Los Barriles, which is outside of the Buena Vista municipality. Los Barriles' fire department was summoned but when the responsible person was located it developed that the fire truck was hors de combat and logically Fito went into action.

Conservative estimates of Fito's velocity when he passed the Pemex station are in the seventy-mile per hour range. As always he was accompanied by his contingent of helmeted twelve-year-olds. While BVFD's immediate response was commendable, much time had been consumed by communication and the fire had mostly died of natural causes. Fito and company laid lines, dispatched smoldering remains with a liberal amount of water and thus created an admirable quantity of white smoke, which informed everyone of Fito's heroic success.

A celebration was in order. BVFD went cruising, picking up passengers of varying ages and varying degrees of sobriety along the way. A *mariachi* band was encountered and given the post of honor atop the fire truck. When the fire truck became saturated with people several pickup trucks joined the procession. The crescendo of *mariachi* music, the siren and pickup horns were not terminated until the wee hours of the subsequent A.M. Local opinion has it that the festivities would have continued had the damned fire truck not run out of gasoline.

BUSH PILOT

The editors are on my ass; "After all Jim, you do have a certain notoriety as a Baja Bush Pilot, and to date, no flying stories have appeared in your manuscript!"

First off, let's see if we can establish a definition as to what in hell is a "Baja Bush Pilot". My old chum Arnold Senterfitt formed a flying club a number of years ago that sort of went along with his airport guidebook to the peninsula. This club was known as "THE BAJA BUSH PILOTS" and was primarily devoted to weekend penetrations of the peninsula. While I carried an honorary membership card for a number of years, I was never a dues-paying member of this club. I did write a little squiggle concerning the founding of the Mission of San Ignacio that appeared in an edition or two of "*Airports of Baja California*". My old sidekick, Dave Deal and I did considerable research for Arnold and went along on some of his group fly-in trips. As my memory serves, Dave also did the layout and artwork for one edition of Arnold's book. Based on this, I must confess that I was indeed a Baja Bush Pilot.

My reasons and purposes for owning, flying and maintaining an aircraft are, and have always been, somewhat out of phase with John Q. Pilot. Aircraft owners and pilots in the land of K-Mart have a love affair with their flying machines that borders on the obscene. They come to Baja California because it is another place to fly. Conversely, this reporter regards an aircraft as a utility vehicle and with about the same function and status as a pickup truck. Haste and the absence of roads oftentimes makes a Cessna more practical than a Toyota. "*Panzita Puerca*" ("Little Dirty Belly", so named for the ever-present oil streaks on her underside) was a very nondescript old Cessna sans upholstery (greasy and bloody cargoes have a way of marring upholstery). Panzita Puerca served well for more than a decade and was known in practically every fish camp and rancho where it was possible to land an airplane.

Missions and cargoes varied. Westbound from San Ignacio to La Bocana, Panzita was loaded with a toolbox and an outboard motor. The cargo on the return leg was a live sea turtle and a dead Mexican. Medical evacuations were numerous and not always successful. Landing and taking off on beaches, dry lakebeds and roads were often necessary. Sometimes bent or broken airplanes resulted.

One of my kookier missions entailed landing a group of bottle hunters on the north beach of Santo Domingo Island. Your reporter is not into bottle hunting but those involved seem most enthusiastic about this endeavor and apparently found some rare specimens of old bottles (one alleged to have a value in excess of five-hundred dollars). Santo Domingo is adjacent to Malarrimo (Scavengers) Beach but inaccessible because high surf prohibits boat landings on the seaward side and one is obliged to cross a vast mud flat on the Scammon's Lagoon side. Boat landings are accomplished with the aid of workers who maintain the marine navigational towers from the salt works but with a great amount of effort. At low tide, the north (seaside) beach makes an acceptable strip but if one tarries, he is obliged to wait for the next tide. The beach above tide line is too soft for aircraft operations. According to plan, we departed Tijuana scheduled to arrive at Santa Domingo at mean low tide. The bottle hunters and their camp were off-loaded onto the beach and expected to be retrieved two days later.

I returned as scheduled. The landing was routine but as I attempted to turn about, the nose strut bent and collapsed in the soft sand and Panzita stood on her nose. This resulted in a very badly bent prop. A radio call to the salt works in Guerrero Negro soon had a rescue boat on the way to retrieve my passengers. Your reporter elected to remain with the airplane until repair parts and tools arrived because unattended damaged aircraft are often vandalized. My departing passengers left me their camp equipment, water and food since it would have been a major effort to carry it across the boggy mud flat on the lee side of the island. Capitán Victor Corral made airdrops containing cigarettes, brandy and books from Exportadora de Sal's Beechcraft each morning during my stay on Santa Domingo.

Days were spent beach combing, reading and studying the vast population of ospreys. The ninth morning after the mishap, I was interrupted by the arrival of Auturo Ayala in a Piper Cub. "Turo" had brought the needed prop and nose strut along with tools to effect a repair. In three hours we were back to the company airstrip at Guerrero Negro.

Back in September 1982 hurricane Paul flopped old Panzita Puerca on her back. The airframe was a write-off. Dave Deal found an airframe for sale in North Carolina. We shipped my engine across country and picked up a prop in Yuma. Dave, Austin Willis and I flew Dave's Cessna 180 to Lake Norman Airpark where we assembled "Panzita Puerca II".

Panzita II served me well for a couple of years. Bureaucratic geniuses began to equate all international movement of private aircraft with narcotics smuggling; an attitude, which resulted in surliness from parties on both sides of the border. This attitude eventually filtered down to local levels.

One morning I landed at Punta Colorada to deliver a case of outboard motor oil and was greeted by six Oaxaca Indians in soldier's uniforms. They all had Colt AR 15s leveled at my gut. I decided to sell my airplane that day.

ABOUT THAT DAMNED CEMENT MIXER!

It must have been in the fall of 1964 that Juan Mitre and Jorge Escudero decided to build a new hotel at Punta Pescadero. They sent me up as construction boss. We had twenty-six employees who were all surnamed Lucero, who all came from the village of Cardonal. Life was pretty primitive up there as the road was destroyed in a hurricane and we had to move everything in by boat. Winter winds came in and the surf action made beach landings by boat impossible for weeks at a time. Chancho Cota and I were living in a little waddle and daub *chosa* at the construction site about two miles from Cardonal. Supply lines were screwed up because of the winds and Chancho and I ran out of food. We were pretty hungry, so we decided to go to Cardonal and look for something to eat. We arrived at the village around 4:00 A.M. and found no movement. No people, no dogs, not even chickens were moving. We thought that some tragedy had occurred and were a bit upset by our surroundings. We went to Samuel Lucero's house and knocked at the door.

When Samuel came out Chancho greeted him: "*Que pasa*?" ("What's happening?")

Samuel replied, "*Nada*" ("Nothing").

"We saw the village was all shut down and thought perhaps something was wrong."

Samuel grinned, "Nothing's wrong, we're just listening to Chucho el Roto (a popular soap opera that ran for about thirty years) on the radio."

Supper was goat stew. Chancho swears I ate three plates.

Chancho remarked later, "Damn, I didn't know that the chickens and dogs of Cardonal were soap opera fans."

My responsibility in the Pescadero Hotel project included logistics. Every few weeks, I was dispatched to La Paz to purchase the material needs for the construction site. While on one of these missions, the manager at Casa Cota saw me ogling a cement mixer in the showroom and tackled me saying, "Jim, if you're interested in that piece of iron, I'll let you have it for cost plus freight. It has been setting there for over three years and you're the first person to show interest in it."

I entertained visions that my crew would be eternally grateful should this machine show up as they were mixing cement with shovels and hoes in the cut-off top of an old Chevy van.

After much pleading with the administration, a purchase order was issued and we became the owners of an iron wheeled, one sack, cement mixer with a Briggs & Stratton gasoline engine.

Juan Rubio's old bread van was used to transport the mixer from La Paz to Los Barriles. Since it would not fit inside the van it was disassembled and transported on top of the van. This created no problem, as the machine had to be broken down to be moved by skiff to Pescadero anyway.

Disembarkation through mild surf at Pescadero was accomplished with much sweating and swearing. Samuel and I reassembled our new toy witnessed by a keenly fascinated audience. Samuel became the engineer and operator because he had demonstrated a certain affinity for machinery. I demonstrated operation techniques by running a couple of loads and asked the crew, "Okay, fellows, got the idea?"

"Yep, we got it nailed."

"Great, then it's your baby. I'm going back to camp for a bite of breakfast."

I returned to the site an hour or so later and found sixteen Luceros sitting around staring at their shoes.

"What's up guys?"

"We're on strike."

"Strike? Why?"

"That damned Machine!"

"Machine? What's wrong with the machine?"

"We don't like it."

"But why?"

"It makes us work too hard!"

The cement mixer was never used again during my tenure at Pescadero. However, I found it behind Playas de Cortez hotel thirty years later and it appeared to be completely worn out.

THE CHANGARRO

Every *barrio* (neighborhood) has at least one *changarro.* Some *barrios* have several. The current rage is to name them *minisuper* but, in local idiom, they are still *changarros. Changarros* are as much a part of the Mexican scene as the tortillas and frijoles that are their stock in trade along with milk, beer, bread, cigarettes, and local gossip.

Most *changarros* are of humble dimensions, usually of less than five hundred square feet. Because of limited floor space, the customer is obliged to order merchandise from outside the store and is served through a window. This space saving arrangement has the added advantage of keeping shoplifting at a minimum.

These are mom and pop operations. Their clientele are repeaters with known purchasing habits, likes and dislikes. A goodly amount of purchasing in a *changarro* is done by children sent by their mothers, therefore, the *changarrero* often has the responsibility of anticipating the wants of the mother since some of the youngsters are five years old (or less) and are developing communication skills.

Locally produced merchandise such as fruits, ranch cheese, hand made tortillas, *chorizo* (homemade pork sausage), dried beef and pastries are supplied by ranchers who cannot write an official receipt that would be accepted by an accountant, therefore, these items are not found in supermarkets, only in *changarros.*

Minisuper Playas del Tesoro is a *changarro* located on Mexico Highway 1 (just south of the Pemex gas station) in Los Barrilles. The proprietress is Señora Guadalupe del Socorro Romero de Smith who is burdened with the dubious honor of being the wife of your reporter. Lupe has been a *changarrera* for some nine years as this is written. She loves it!

My own true love initiated a campaign to become a retailer some twenty years past when we returned to Mexico from Saudi Arabia. I was able to resist this insane urge until we purchased a residence facing Highway 1, an ideal business location. I anticipated that Lupe would bankrupt and/or become bored within sixty days and was therefore not motivated to invest much in the proposed enterprise. A small structure (14' x 22') was erected from lumber intended for another purpose. Tecate Beer Company supplied paint. Lupe was in business! It was then I discovered that my wife is one of the most aggressive retail merchants in the Republic of Mexico.

Minisuper Playas del Tesoro's function as a mercantile enterprise has become coincidental to being a social center, news bureau, political headquarters and rumor mill. Subjects discussed by Doña Lupe and her customers range from profound to mundane (she and Doña Cuca Sandez were once observed discussing the relative merits of one tomato for two minutes twenty-two seconds). It is from here, the *changarro*, that Lupe benevolently rules our *barrio*.

My function? I carry out the trash and restock the beer coolers!

COCO

Coco is Mexican, born in the sovereign Republic of Mexico on the last day of July of the Year of Our Lord 1970. Her mother is a native of a small village in the central desert of Baja California. Her father is a globetrotting itinerant gringo pilot and mechanic but will engage in any other legal endeavor that seems lucrative at the moment.

She wandered about the world with Mom and Dad, picked up a couple of extra languages and returned to her native Baja California in the summer of her eleventh year. She entered her first Mexican school in La Ribera. She tried to read and write in English and/or Arabic. She spoke Spanish fluently but had never seen it on paper. The teacher deemed her the most hopeless case known throughout the entire republic.

Fortunately, Dad changed jobs and Coco moved to another school. Professor Oscar Olechea, at Buena Vista Rural School, recognized the problem immediately. When Coco finished her primary studies, she graduated as valedictorian and was automatically chosen to represent her school in the state interscholastic competition held in Los Planes that year.

Each candidate appeared in Los Planes with the director of their school. They were to complete an exam of one hundred-twenty questions within three hours. The winner of this contest, along with his or her mother, was awarded a trip to Mexico City to have breakfast with President Miguel de la Madrid and the First Lady, Paloma.

Two hours and forty minutes from the starting gun, Coco arose, and handed her completed exam to the monitoring professor. The monitor asked, "Is this complete?"

Coco replied, "Yes sir, it is complete."

"You still have twenty minutes. Return to your seat and bring your exam at the end of three hours," ordered the teacher.

Coco complied and handed in her exam paper at the end of three hours. She sat outside alone for almost an hour before the next candidate appeared. The last candidates finished their exams something around four and a half hours from starting. Professor Oscar Olechea was rabid.

The papers were graded. Coco had answered one hundred nineteen questions correctly. A certain young lady from Santiago had answered all one hundred twenty questions correctly but had exceed the allotted time by one hour and ten minutes. All hell broke loose. Professor Olechea was defending his candidate to the death while the kids sat on benches outside in the sun and listened to their stomachs growl.

No way, no how was Baja California about to send a student with a name like Wilma Smith to represent their state at a breakfast with the president. Coco (age twelve) recognized this fact. She meekly entered the salon where the learned professors were conducting their heated argument. "Ladies and Gentleman," she said, "I know you have a problem. I have been talking to the other candidate and she tells me that she has never been farther from her home than La Paz. I have had breakfast in London, Paris, Rome, Bangkok, New York and Los Angeles. Please, let her have breakfast with Miguel de la Madrid so we can have lunch in Los Planes."

Six weeks after the young lady from Santiago returned from her Mexico City sojourn, a delegation from the state department of education appeared at Coco's home. "We have reevaluated the test scores and are declaring you the winner. Please accept this certificate which designates that you won the state educational competition."

"Bigoted sirs," retorted Coco, "I knew I had won the contest the moment I handed my paper to the monitor. I suggest you take your certificate and put it where the sun doesn't shine."

Coco has recently completed her PADI scuba diver instructor's course in record time. She can be found at Agua Deportes on the beach in front of Hacienda Hotel. I'm very proud of her. She is my youngest daughter.

THE TRAGEDY OF CONCEPCIÓN ARGUELLO

Shortly after founding the Russian colony of Sitka in Alaska in1799, the colonists appealed to the Czar for relief, as they were dying from starvation and scurvy. Russian nobleman Niokolia Resanov was dispatched from St. Petersburg to inspect conditions in Alaska and try to acquire necessary supplies for Sitka. He arrived to discover that this settlement was in dire need of assistance. Fortunately, the American ship Juno put in at the port. Resanov bought the ship and the entire cargo. He soon set sail for California searching for additional food for the Sitka Russians.

Resanov sailed the Juno into San Francisco Bay on April 5, 1806. He anchored and dispatched his naturalist, surgeon and friend, Doctor George Heinrich Von Lagsdorff. Since Dr. Von Lagsdorff spoke no Spanish and no one ashore spoke Russian, the priest was located and conversation was conducted in Latin.

Spanish regulations existing at that time prohibited commerce with foreigners, but the Californio's curiosity and generous nature won out. The Russians were allowed to land and were received with hospitality. Resanov was entertained in the home of the port commander, José Dario Arguello. The visitors were impressed with the happy, well-fed lifestyle of the Californios. Most of all, they were impressed by the gaiety, the beauty and the lively nature of the California women.

Commander Arguello's sixteen-year-old daughter, Concepción (Conchita) was known as the most vivacious and prettiest *muchacha* in all the Californias. Resanov was immediately smitten and courted Conchita with ardor. Conchita was charmed by his tales of the Czar in St. Petersburg and a romance soon blossomed. Resanov soon proposed marriage and Conchita accepted. The priests promised to petition the Pope for the girl to marry outside her faith (normally foreign bridegrooms were required to be baptized into the Catholic faith as a condition of marriage).

Resanov procured a shipload of flour, peas, beans and dried beef and prepared to return to Sitka. He attempted to forge a firm contract for future trade with California's Governor, José Juaquin Arillaga. After much haggling, Arillaga passed the buck and promised to forward the request to his superiors. Since the trade was illegal, it is most doubtful that this request was dispatched.

Resanov planned to deliver the supplies to Sitka and return to Russia. From Russia his itinerary included visits to Spain and Mexico before returning to California for his wedding to Conchita. It is assumed his globe trotting had to do with chasing permits to marry (FM3?).

Resanov delivered the Juno and her cargo to Sitka and started his long trek to St. Petersburg across Siberia. En route, he became ill with fever and exhaustion. He suffered a fall from his horse and died. Conchita heard nothing from or about her fiancé and, therefore, ignored advances from many suitors.

José Dario Arguello went up the political ladder and was appointed governor of Lower California at Loreto in 1814. It must be assumed that Conchita accompanied him since it is recorded that Captain James Smith Wilcox arrived in Loreto aboard his ship Traveler with a cargo of wheat consigned to that port and made valiant efforts to marry the now twenty-seven year old Conchita. He was spurned, as she was still waiting for Resanov.

When next heard from, Conchita Arguello had returned from Loreto and entered the Dominican order as a nun in Monterey, "Alta California", still ignorant of Resanov's fate.

In 1842 Sir George Simpson, governor of the Hudson Bay Company, visited Monterey. At a banquet in his honor, Conchita learned what happened to her lover when some one mentioned Resanov. The occasion was commemorated by a poem by Bret Harte:

"Quickly then," cried Sir George Simpson
"Speak no ill of him, I pray!
He is dead. He died poor fellow, forty years
Ago this day.
Left a sweetheart, too they tell me. Married, I
Suppose of course!
Lives she yet?" A deathlike silence fell
On banquet, guests, and hall.
And a trembling figure rising fixed the
Awe struck gaze of all.

The black eyes in darkened orbits gleamed
Beneath the nun's white hood;
Black serge hid the wasted figure, bowed and
Stricken where it stood.
"Lives she yet?" Sir George repeated. All were
Hushed as Conchita drew
Closer yet her nun's attire. "Señor, pardon, she
Died, too!"

Conchita Arguello is reported to have died in a Dominican convent in Monterey at age sixty-six. You can view a figure of her in the wax museum located on Cannery Row. Blow her a kiss for me when you visit.

CONCERNING PIGS

Bob Van Wormer was manager of Hotel Bahía de Palmas (now known as Hotel Palmas de Cortez) in the days of yore. One night it came to Bob's attention that a vagrant porker was happily engaged in destroying the hotel landscape. Bob, intending no bodily harm, cranked off a round from a twelve-gauge shotgun in an effort to scare the intruder. No wounds were observed, leading Bob to conclude that the pig's death was a result of a massive coronary. In Bob's assessment, some of the more discriminating guests might take offense to a dead hog in the hotel patio. He, therefore, elected to conceal the *corpus delicti* under an upturned boat on the beach. Bob Van Wormer is hardly the criminal type. However, on this occasion he was doubtlessly motivated by the belief that the swine was property of Antonio Verdugo. Señor Verdugo's sentiments regarding a gringo fishing resort encroaching on his private domain were ill concealed. (It should be noted however, that as this is written the entire descendants of Señor Verdugo are fat and sleek from tourist related enterprises.)

Bob chose to give the pig the old cement overcoat treatment. Frank Van Wormer, Dr. Cliff Francisco and Olen Berger became co-conspirators in the crime at breakfast that morning and agreed to tow the evidence out to sea. Rumor of a sierra mackerel run in front of the tuna hole reached Frank and Cliff as they were launching their boat and the pig towing expedition was shelved. They reasoned that pig disposal could be accomplished at their leisure but the sierra would not wait. In their haste, they overlooked an important item - fuel. Frank and Cliff soon found themselves adrift around the tuna hole as the pig cadaver simmered under a boat on the beach.

Meanwhile, back at the ranch, Bob and Berger put the evidence in a gunny sack along with a goodly number of rocks (for weight, you know) and awaited the return of the wayward sierra fishermen. Several hours elapsed. Bob and Berger launched an air search mission, but went in the wrong direction. The aircraft's return to Palmas was simultaneous with that of the boat bearing Frank and Cliff. Sunset was coming when the porker was finally committed to "Davie Jones Locker."

Several weeks subsequent to these events, Bob observed Chapo Tomayo, obviously in the search mode, on the beach in front of Palmas Hotel. When queried, Chapo said that he was looking for a missing pig and suspected that Pilar Cota had barbecued same. Bob confessed his sin to Chapo and paid a fair price.

Bob Van Warmer doesn't have an exclusive on pig altercations. A certain Mr. Jones fell victim to the real estate ads and erected his little corner of heaven up near Aqua de la Costa. Mr. Jones vainly tried to explain his privacy rights to one of Don Manuel Gonzales' porkers. The pig was not impressed. Numerous pleas to the Gonzales family were also unproductive. One of Señor Gonzales' sons became bored with Mr. Jones' complaints and suggested that perhaps Mr. Jones should resort to defending his property physically. Mr. Jones interpreted this suggestion literally and when the pig reappeared, Mr. Jones defended his domicile with a spear gun, resulting in porkicide.

Don Manuel Gonzales received due payment, the locals at Aqua de la Costa enjoyed a pig roast and "*Mata Coche*" Jones was christened with a nickname that will doubtlessly be engraved on his headstone. "*Mata Coche*" translates into "Pig Killer."

DAVID MOISES

Today, September 9, 1996, my number one son, Raul and his wife, Lupita, pridefully arrived at my residence with their latest acquisition: David *Moises* (Moses).

Moises had no idea of what was going on here as he has reached the vast age of about twenty-eight days and his only concerns were, "When is my next meal coming?" and "Will you people leave me alone so I can get some sleep?"

Did I fail to mention that David Moises is an infant Homo sapiens? Yes, he is a baby boy, not particularly attractive at this age but one never knows how he will evolve.

David Moises has had some pretty rough sledding considering his tender age. He was abandoned in San Lucas shortly after his birth and became a ward of the state.

We will not pass judgment on his mother and father for we have no knowledge of their motivations.

The bottom line here is; this dude needed some help. That's where Raul and Lupita entered the picture.

They allegedly considered all factors; they live in a little two-bedroom *Fornatur* (government subsidized) house out on the Todos Santos Highway and already have three kids. Things are going to be a bit crowded but damn it, David Moises needs a home!

Raul and Lupita adopted David Moises.

They came over today to show me my new grandson.

Raul queried, "What do you think, pop?"

And I replied, "You're either the noblest or the dumbest bastard I have ever seen and damned if I know which."

"Pop," exclaimed Raul, "You've forgotten that I am also adopted!"

He was right, I had forgotten.

DILEMMAS OF A NOVICE RESEARCHER

Crosby, Mathis, Aschmann, Gerhard, Wheelock, Martinez, Reyes, Williams, Ewing, Roberts, Dunne, Pourade and many other scholars of Baja California history list *Observations in Lower California* by Padre Johann Jakob Baegert SJ as a research reference. This passage appears in the second paragraph of the first chapter:

"The aforementioned Red River is, of all the waters which empty into the almost four-hundred-hour-long California Ocean, the only one that deserves to be called "river," and near California it is more than a quarter of an hour wide. All others found on the maps are hardly more than rain-water courses, which during the greater part of the year have very little water, so that it is possible to ride through them without wetting ones shoes. However, in all of them abide alligators of considerable size, and since some of them are capable of devouring a full-grown man, it is necessary to be on guard while drawing water, bathing or washing. I have seen several of these creatures. As everyone knows, they resemble a lizard, but are completely clad in armor like a turtle. Not many years ago it was discovered in America that the eyeteeth of alligators are a strong antidote. By applying to the wound or swallowing some of the powder scraped from the teeth, the lives of many who have been bitten by snakes have been saved."

While this writer (as yet unpublished) in no way pretends to be of a scholarly bent, the above statement causes me to wonder if perhaps the Guaycura medicine men at San Luis Gonzaga introduced Father Baegert to the joys of smoking jimson weed.

Another burr under my saddle blanket concerns Ildefanso Green's rifle on display at the Regional Museum in La Paz. Professor Reyes' pamphlet on the life of Ildefanso Green lists it as a .50 caliber Mauser. I have been to the Museum twice. One curator tells me that it is .32-20 while another assures me the gun is a .30 caliber. Steven Chisum, our resident gunsmith in Los Barriles, finds this most curious since Mauser only manufactured these arms in one caliber - 7mm.

1
It was a dark and stormy night
Somewhere a rooster went
Caca Doodle Doo!
Yeah! Right.......................
-(30)-
UNDERWOOD
POLICE
BALDWIN PAR
SINGER
FOR MY MUY
ESTIMADO
COMPADRE
J.F. SMITH JR.
ALIAS THE
GRINNING GARGOYLE
DAVE 'BIG DEAL'

Professor Pablo L. Martinez, in *Baja California Family Guide,* lists the birth of the above mentioned Baja California hero, Ildefanso Cipriano Green Ceseña, in San José del Cabo on 23 January 1836. Martinez also records that Green died in 1932 at ninety-six years of age. Professor Leonardo Reyes Silva, in his pamphlet *De la Reforma a la Revolution con Ildefanso Green*, reports that Green was born on 23 January 1830 and that he lived to be one hundred two years old. In 1930, Green spoke about his life experiences on what he alleged to be his one-hundredth birthday. The transcript of this oration is in files of the archives at the Theatro de la Cuidad in La Paz. Green's headstone on his grave at the rotunda near the Theatro de la Ciudad lists his birthday as 23 January 1830. Martinez states that Green's mother (Jesúsa Ceseña) was born in 1820 which would have made her about 10 years old at the time of Ildefanso's birth. Martinez also records that Steven Green (Ildefonso's father) did not arrive in Baja California until 1834.

I was bemoaning this conflict to Socorro Gonzales, one of the librarians in the Pablo Martinez Archives. "Co" answered, "That's the problem with you gringos, Jim, you're just too damned precise."

THE CONQUEST OF DOÑA LUPE

The Mexican courtship is a complex ritual indeed, incomprehensible to those of other cultures. The faux pas of strangers intent on committing matrimony with the village princess of an upland pueblo of Baja California are legendary. Oftentimes penalties incurred for some social blunder can be compared to Parcheesi. Should one omit certain necessary steps in the ritual, he is obligated to return to square one.

First off, the suitor must prove his social status. The old Spanish caste system is alive and well in these waters and strictly enforced. The village princess' regal state in these small remote pueblos is based on various factors, principally family wealth and bloodline. Assuming the target of our hero's affections has some stature in the community, he will be obligated to demonstrate that he is of equal or superior station to that enjoyed by the intended bride. Since our candidate is of an unknown quality, he will be required to spend some time in the community to present evidence that he is worthy. Apart from these requisites, the candidate must display his physical attractiveness as well as a pleasing personality.

Your reporter was totally ignorant of the above listed data when the courtship of Guadalupe Romero Lopez was initiated at San Ignacio, Baja California, in the spring of 1953.

Doña Lupe will describe our first encounter:

"I was engaged in some unremembered activity in the kitchen when I heard a very loud and rude noise in the street in front of our house. Investigation revealed that some sort of humanoid had arrived at the gas pump in front of Meza's store. He was clad from head to foot in black leather. His head was covered with a white object resembling a chamber pot. He had apparently been transported on a two wheeled conveyance that I later learned is called a motorcycle. He attempted to converse in a guttural and unintelligible language, which proved to be English. After his failure to make himself understood, he did the most astounding thing. He sat on the concrete base of the gas pump, removed one of his boots and exhibited his bare foot. This foot was swollen and discolored. Those present concluded that he was trying to tell us he was injured! I moved nearer to examine the injury and he committed a horrible act...he winked at me!!"

The alleged chamber pot was a new Bell 500 helmet that had set me back sixty bucks! I was trying to communicate that my foot had suffered severely in an altercation with a rock and a fracture was suspected. Yes, I did wink at that cute little trick, never dreaming that in the local idiom this amounted to an outright proposition.

Guero Soldado, the local expert in English and tequila, appeared after a bit and reported that no doctor was available but a local healer could perhaps be of some help.

Lodgings were found at Casa Leree, the local *pension* (boarding house) and the *curandero* was summoned. The healer applied a liberal amount of Vick's Vaporub to the ailing foot and pulled on my toes until I yelled. He sold me a bottle of bootleg mescal, locally called *pecho amarillo* (yellow chest) and departed.

Guero remained at my bedside and expressed his sympathy by consuming a lion's share of the liter of *pecho amarillo*. When the mescal supply ran out, Guero reported that he could procure more if I could supply twenty pesos. Shortly after Guero's departure, I decided I had been conned out of twenty pesos and went to sleep. This proved to be untrue. A well-nibbled bottle of *pecho amarillo* was present and accounted for when I awoke to the noise of a revving motorcycle engine. Suspicion that my motorcycle was being stolen proved to be unfounded. Jack Mulcahy arrived. Like me, he was traveling by bike and had been pursuing me since Ensenada.

Jack reported that a dance was in progress nearby and expressed a desire to attend. He remedied my ailing foot with a pair of codeine pain pills and a goodly supply of *pecho amarillo*. We cleaned our leather riding togs, brought them up to a sheen with Brilteen hair oil and mounted our steeds in search of nightlife.

Our arrival at the *baile* (dance) created a sensation. The merrymakers insisted we bring the bikes into the dance hall where the light afforded better inspection. As the evening progressed, several young ladies present donned our helmets, mounted the motorbikes and uttered simulated engine noises much to the delight of the onlookers. The dance ended late.

The next morning, the excruciating throb in my cranium was exceeded by a kindred sensation in my left foot. It seems I had spent the evening and wee hours dancing on a fractured pedal digit resulting in a swollen and discolored foot that would not fit into a three-gallon bucket. A liberal supply of Leree's coffee ad Mulcahy's codeine soon made life tolerable.

Mulcahy alleged fluency in the local idiom when I expressed a desire to develop an acquaintance with a certain young lady observed at Meza's gas pump the previous day. He proved to be most resourceful. He soon supplied a crutch and we set out to visit the señorita.

Here, once again, we will let Doña Lupe supply the narrative:

"You can imagine my horror when this same gringo appeared at my home that morning with a companion who spouted gibberish that he apparently believed to be the Spanish language. My mother invited them into the kitchen and served them coffee! I hid in a bedroom. After a long effort to communicate, they left. My mother reported that while she was not certain, she believed that he gringo with the broken foot had come to ask for my hand. I will not repeat my father's remarks about this development."

Square one minus five!

Mulcahy departed to the south after a couple of days, leaving me to my own adventures in San Ignacio, immobilized with a broken foot.

Around that time, lobster fisherman returned from the coast with money in their pockets. San Ignacio would be in the fiesta mode. Music was heard at all hours. The fishermen had time on their hands and much to their amusement, set out to teach the gringo the rudiments of the idiom. I could swear with the best before I conjugated my first verb. After considerable coaching, my first attempt at dialog with my intended went somewhat askew: "Que bonitas nalgas tiene usted!"("What a lovely ass you have.")

Square one minus ten!

As spring waned into summer, my foot healed. I explored the fishing camps on the Pacific, the Viscaíno Desert and the Sierra San Francisco. I could detect no progress in my courtship of Guadalupe.

Diminishing finances compelled temporary abandonment of my pursuit for Señorita Romero.

I was back on station in San Ignacio in March 1954 with my pockets lined with pesos and armed with a certain linguistic ability gained at the adult education facility of the Long Beach public school system. Guadalupe was not impressed. A certain Señor Rocha had captured her attention and all her free time was spent on a park bench in the plaza gazing soulfully into Señor Rocha's eyes.

I employed various and sundry ruses to renew my imagined conquest with the result that I made a complete ass of myself.

My summer was spent murdering boll weevils in the cotton fields of west Texas from a Piper Cub. There, a new plan was formed. Since airplane pilots enjoy a special status in Mexico, the motorcycle would be shelved and my next attack would be by aircraft! My sensational arrival at San Ignacio in a shiny new rented Cessna during the subsequent spring was noted by the entire populous save one; Guadalupe Romero Lopez.

Since Señor Rocha had ridden off into the sunset, Lupe was a free agent. My linguistic skills had improved sufficiently at this point to give me the confidence to propose marriage without the aid of an interpreter. Her answer was one of the few words that English and Spanish have in common; No!

My parting shot was, "Very well, m' love. I'll return next spring for another go."

And I did! I returned and proposed each spring until 1968. That year, her betrothed would not release his grip on her hand long enough for me to say more than hello. After fifteen consecutive unsuccessful tries, the effort was abandoned.

The spring of 1969 found me with time on my hands. I had recently returned from a civilian job in Vietnam and had to spend some three months outside the USA to escape income taxes. Old habits die-hard. After a leisurely trip down the peninsula, I was once again in San Ignacio.

While superhuman effort was required, I concealed my delight on learning that the1968- model suitor had ridden into the same sunset as Señor Rocha.

A sinister plot was afoot. Hilda and Abel Aguilar invited me to a dinner party to celebrate my return. My assumption that this would be a quiet affair proved to be untrue. A goodly number of people, including Guadalupe, were present. Dancing followed dinner. I adopted the posture of a bored spectator until Guadalupe approached and asked,

"Will you dance with me?"

We danced in silence for a time.

"Will you ask me to marry again this year?" she queried to my amazement.

"I think not!" said I. A man has his pride!

"Very well then, I will ask. Will you marry me?"

Guadalupe and I have nine grandchildren as of this writing!

DRESS CODE

About the only consistency one can observe from periodic articles concerning this writer is: "JIM SMITH WEARS COVERALLS." This is true.

Am I violating some contemporary dress code?

Since I have been out of contact with the "real world" for more years than can be counted, could it be that I am unaware of some grave faux pas that should be corrected?

This same problem existed in Saudi Arabia. As a titled executive, one is expected to appear at his desk in uniform. As a concession to the climate, tropical suits were permitted. The man who made this law did not have my case in mind as my responsibility entailed frequent close contact with large diesel powered fire fighting apparatuses and earth moving equipment. Seersucker suits didn't work out worth a damn in this environment. I wore the only coveralls available; bright orange for visibility around high density traffic areas on the airport ramps. These orange coveralls were intended for use by janitorial personnel. The administration felt that it was unbefitting my status to parade up and down executive row in janitor's coveralls. The final solution to this problem was presented to a Bond Street tailor who created executive "boiler suits" much like those worn by Winston Churchill. The expense was born by my employer.

K-Mart supplies me with summer weight, six pocket, zippered coveralls. The current nomenclature, JUMP SUIT, is confusing. Are they intended for parachuting or seducing damsels? I suspect the later as the zippers facilitate hasty exit (disrobing) and entry (robing).

Why coveralls? COMFORT, dear reader, PURE SOLID COMFORT. Try 'em!

EAST CAPE ESCAPE

The serenity of the sandy shores of Bahía de Palmas has not suffered appreciably considering the phenomenal growth of tourist facilities that has occurred in the last fifteen years. Seven resorts located here on the East Cape feature big game fishing unduplicated in the entire world yet maintain the tranquil ambiance that has prevailed over the centuries. Some two hundred American-owned homes are located here, but since the perimeter of the bay is something around thirty miles, everyone has plenty of elbowroom.

Los Barriles and Buena Vista are, for all purposes, one village of about eighteen-hundred souls. The county line runs between the villages - hence two names. This is a little confusing to the casual visitor but causes the local populace no concern except on election day. (Doña Rosa Flores has a real problem with this because her kitchen is in Los Cabos county and her bedroom is in La Paz County.)

While sport fishing is the mainstay of tourism on the East Cape, wind surfing (in season from November through March) and diving (both snorkeling and scuba) cannot be ignored as contributors to the local economy.

Sport fishing boat crews are local people and have spent a lifetime chasing marlin, sailfish, dorado, roosterfish and wahoo in these waters. They have no peers.

Hotel personnel now occupy the same posts as their fathers and mothers and demonstrate pride in their work. Their primary concern is the comfort and contentment of the guests who are treated as honored family members rather than customers.

Other facilities catering the needs of the visitor are: five restaurants, two supermarkets, public phone and FAX, two real estate offices for those who elect to stay, two property management companies to accommodate those who wish to lease a house for a few months, and several building contractors. Six trailer parks accommodate the needs of the mobile home faction.

The one glaring deficiency on the East Cape is nightlife. Sidewalks would be rolled up at 10 P.M., if we had sidewalks. What we deal in here is TRANQUILLITY.

Drop in for a visit!

ED PEARLMAN

Strange as it may seem, the multi-billion dollar tourist industry in Baja California Sur owes it's existence to a kooky scheme hatched by a San Fernando Valley florist.

Tourism below the twenty-eighth parallel amounted to a few sport-fishing resorts in Mulegé, Loreto, La Paz, East Cape and Cape San Lucas in 1967. The resorts were almost exclusively the domain of the private aviation crowd and received very little exposure apart from publications slanted toward sport fishing and private aviation. Overland tourist traffic was limited to a few hardy individuals, with specialized fields of interest, and equipped with specialized vehicles.

Exaggerated yarns appearing in motorcycling magazines stirred the imagination of the sales department of American Honda Motorcycle Company and they set out to establish an elapsed time record from the border to La Paz. *Argosy Magazine* published an account of this "time-trial" which was more fiction than fact but at least it got some ink out and resulted in a number of attempts to best the alleged record by both riders of bikes and four wheel vehicles. Poole and Murray established one of the most incredible of these record claims in a street stock Rambler Sedan.

Ed Pearlman, the Valley florist, decided that an all out race from Tijuana to La Paz was in order. The initial "Mexican 1000 Off Road Race" attracted less than sixty entries and had the aura of a club event rather than a major international race. Don Francisco, an old publicity head in the automotive racing scene, did his job well and the resulting coverage was overwhelming.

The Madison Avenue boys who handled the Chevrolet truck publicity staged a leisurely caravan (complete with mechanics, spare parts and a machine shop) down to La Paz and turned the resulting footage over to copywriters who came up with some of the most nauseating copy since the "*I LOVE LUCY SHOW*." They proclaimed **"WE BEAT THE BAJA,"** on national television! Those individuals who had an intimate acquaintanceship with Baja California wonder where in hell "**THE BAJA**" is located. While "**THE BAJA**" has become a household word with those who spend thirty percent of their time in front of a television, it still sends cold chills up the spines of the people who know and love the peninsula.

The news that Baja California had the worst road in the Western Hemisphere reached President Luis Echeverría Álvarez and his regime in Mexico's capital city via NBC and CBS. Until this time, they had regarded Baja California as the Mexican Republic's Pacific hemorrhoid. Their national pride had been ground to dust under the heels of General Motors, in their view, and they soon started construction on a trans-peninsular highway.

Mexico Highway 1 was completed in 1973. The old Mexican 1000 was renamed The Baja 1000 (that goddamned name again) and attracted sponsorship from major automobile and motorcycle manufacturers. It became a major international racing event complete with professional drivers and network television coverage.

Major hotel chains knew good publicity when they saw it and started construction. International airport development was a natural spin-off as was a major effort to cultivate tourism. God only knows where it will eventually end.

Perhaps tourism would have developed through other natural channels, who knows?

Ed Pearlman? When last heard from, he was still selling carnations.

EL BRUJO (The Wizard)

Mechanic: **n**. 1) a worker skilled in using tools or making,operating, and repairing machines. 2) an artisan; handicraftsman,especially one who repairs machines.

*Webster's New World Dictionary

Fred Velasco, while performing all of the above, somehow manages to elevate the menial title of mechanic to a high art. Fred compliments the above job description with design, fabrication, assembly, experimentation, imagination and an attitude that nothing is impossible.

Fred discovered that automatic transmission repair was a facet missing from his skills. He approached his employer, stating that perhaps he should attend an automatic transmission repair school. Investigation revealed that the only automatic transmission schools were in the USA and classes there were only taught in the English language. First things being first, Fred learned English in a matter of a few months and off to auto trans school he went.

Before he decided to go out on his own, Fred served as chief mechanic for Rancho Buena Vista. After leaving Rancho Buena Vista, he opened a repair shop and parts store in downtown Los Barriles.

One afternoon a highland rancher arrived at Fred's shop and announced, "*Maestro*, I come that you may revise my truck."

Fred approached the old Ford cautiously, untied the rope that secured the hood, lifted the hood and propped it open with a handy stick. He gazed in amazement into Dante's Inferno. The battery terminals were great gobs of green goop; the carburetor was a malignant mass of mutable mud. The radiator did not leak; it wept. A tarry substance that might have been motor oil at one time seeped from every conceivable seam. Battery caps, oil filter cap, radiator cap, air cleaner and dipstick were conspicuously absent. The fan belt functioned only by a Catholic miracle (something to do with a statuette of the Virgin of Guadalupe affixed to the dashboard, I'm sure).

"By the sainted penis of Judas," he said in amazement.

He stood at rigid attention while he sang the Mexican National Anthem in a *basso profundo*, ceremoniously made the sign of the cross over the engine compartment, closed the hood and neatly re-knotted the rope that secured the hood.

"Sir," said Velasco, "Your truck has been revised."

"What do I owe you?" asked the rancher.

"On the house."

"God will pay you," said the rancher as he mounted the truck and drove away.

Damned if I don't believe the truck ran better when the rancher left!

EL MORO'S BEQUEST

El Moro marched into the Los Cabos scene to the syncopated beat of his own special drummer. He was accompanied by two huge Rottweilers, a pair of eight foot red tailed Colombian boa constrictors, a Zulu princess (his description) and a desire to write. His journalistic endeavors were somewhat dampened by an ultra-liberal attitude, blue language and vindictiveness. El Moro was forced to engage in more lucrative pursuits; he stalked unsuspecting pilgrims on the streets of San Lucas and, by some magic process, the pilgrim became the owner of a time-share condo. El Moro had found his forte. His escalation in the time-share company was ballistic which resulted in a transfer to Cancun.

Habitation in Cancun for the Zulu princess and the Rottweilers was duly acquired. The boas presented a problem, however, and were left in Buena Vista in the care of a snake sitter who somehow allowed the male to escape. El Moro was advised of this development and returned to Buena Vista to search for his vagrant serpent. After several days, El Moro declared the snake hunt as useless and packed the female boa in a handbag. It is unknown if the handbag was carry-on or checked baggage for the airline trip to Cancun.

Last evening a certain Mr. G returned to his beachfront home from a fishing trip. Mr. G's plan to utilize his outside shower before entering the house was aborted when it was discovered that the missing boa had established residence inside. Several stalwart friends were recruited, each with their theory of how the capture should be expedited. The snake beat a hasty retreat under a freezer. The freezer was summarily moved and the snake adopted a defensive posture emitting an admirable amount of hisses. One stalwart snake hunter found refuge atop the bathroom commode while the remaining ad-libbed their individual escapes. Our heroes persevered and ultimately the boa was housed in a gunnysack.

Therein lies the problem. Wives and red tailed Colombian boas are not compatible, but putting this jungle-bred critter on his own recognizance in the Baja California desert would seal his doom. El Moro can't be located. Any suggestions?

IT'S ABOUT THE FEDERAL ZONE

Mexican law is fairly specific in regard to beach usage. A zone twenty meters from the mean high annual tide is designated as federal property and access for all citizens is guaranteed. Simple? No!

First off, storms (especially at the mouth of an arroyo) and currents cause a fluctuation of the width of the beach. A house constructed well in back of the federal zone may be in violation some time in the future. Conversely, a house constructed at the limit of the federal zone is sometimes located quite a distance inland. It all depends on the whims of nature.

On the East Cape, this law has been modified by the Maritime Secretariat and beaches were leased to the resorts that found their structures located within the federal zone on those years that Ma Nature decided to move some sand. As time passed, the law was again modified, granting exclusive use of the beach to resorts. Foot traffic to the general public was still guaranteed.

Another law prohibiting motor vehicular traffic in the Federal Zone has been on the books historically but enforcement has been very lax.

ATV's became popular about fifteen years ago and since enforcement in the federal zone was non existent, the federal zone became an ATV freeway. This resulted in two or three ATVs in practically all foreign owned residences in Los Barriles and Buena Vista. Everybody rode them; grandpa, grandma, teenyboppers and all possible variances were running up and down the beach on their Hondas.

Guests registered complaints to resort management and a barricade was erected at one of the resorts. This almost caused a war. The constabulary reluctantly intervened and is now issuing warnings in the Buena Vista area. Some foreign beachfront residents have gotten on the bandwagon also and erected barricades.

Outraged ATV owners are bemoaning the fact that they are now forced to use the highway. They report that they feel endangered in the heavy bus and truck traffic. Most of the ATV's are unregistered and are probably in violation on the highway anyway.

Life here on Palmas Bay was much simpler when we had only six gringos, no highway, and no ATV's.

A FIESTA IN SAN JOSÉ DE GRACIA

It must have been around thirty years ago that Guero Soldado and I returned from Sierra Santa Clara to San Ignacio from one of our lost mission huntin' trips. We arrived to find a group of dignitaries (mayor included) from San José de Gracia waiting for us under the grape arbor in Doña Beca Carillo's patio.

These dignitaries had traveled some sixty miles over impossible roads in an old Studebaker pickup to invite me to the annual fiesta, which occurs in San José de Gracia on March 19. I was somewhat flattered until they dropped the other shoe. "Please come on your motorcycle. Our children have never seen a motorcycle or a gringo."

Needless to say, I attended.

Never was a head of state afforded more pomp and ceremony than that which occurred on my arrival at San José de Gracia's plaza. Beautiful little girls in white frocks bearing armloads of brilliant bougainvillea blossoms, the fiesta queen and her court dressed in satin gowns, a uniformed *mariachi* band, the entire populace of San José and surrounding *ranchos* and a long winded speech by the mayor welcomed a dust covered creature clad in black leather and mounted on an unknown two wheeled contraption from the Nippon Empire. This was for openers.

I soon learned that my ever-present sleeping bag was unnecessary. A suite awaited me. My itinerary read something like: breakfast at the residence of Fulano, lunch with Sutano, dinner with Mengano.

Should I choose to dance, my card was full; Señorita Fulano, Señora Sutano, Señorita Mengano and last but not least, Señora Merengano.

Conversation with the organizers soon revealed that in the event that I should find it in my heart to take the local populace for a motorcycle ride, a drawing had been held and a dignitary (appointed for this purpose) would enforce the resulted schedule.

Three subsequent days passed like a kaleidoscope, dancing, eating, drinking and giving motorcycle rides. For a finale, I spun a couple of brodies in the plaza and did a ramp jump over the irrigation canal while departing for San Ignacio.

Duane Culberson and I were goofing around the Salina Cuarenta country last spring and decided to drop into San José de Gracia for a few hours. The old speech makin' *delegado* has been pushin' up daisies for something over twenty years. The satin-gowned fiesta queen and her lovely court are all grandmothers now and the bougainvillea bearing *chamacitas* are mothers of little ones even more beautiful.

They still remember. They say, "Oh yes, I remember you. You were the man on the very first motorcycle I ever saw!"

GABRIELA

Gabriela was of the order *perissodactyle*, family *Equidae* and specifically a *L. asinus* and descended from the first animal to be domesticated as a beast of burden. Hell, Gabriela never was convinced she was a burro and not a Homo sapiens.

Her association with the naked ape began with a tragedy. Jack and Maria Larson were returning to their home on the beach in Buena Vista at a rather late hour when Gabriela's mother became involved in a right of way dispute with Jack's pick-up truck resulting in an orphaned *burrita.*

Marie's maternal compassion overrode logic and Gabriela became a member of the Larson household. Jack was forced to seek a wholesale outlet for Carnation Condensed Milk and daily romps on the beach and a swim with Maria and the dog soon became a ritual.

As Gabriela matured her diet included such staples as cigarettes, gumdrops, peanuts, alfalfa, beer and on certain occasions tequila. She mooched indiscriminately from all that ventured in and around the Larson household and protested with a bray that could not be ignored when slighted.

One of Gabriela's favorite people was an old drunk remembered only as Don Manuel who lived in a *choza* (hut) a short distance from the Larsons. There was no doubt when Don Manuel had scored another bottle of tequila. He dragged out his trusty guitar and Gabriela would join him in front of the *choza* for a few nips, and a duet of revolutionary ballads always ensued. Local opinion was that Gabriela had a better singing voice than Don Manuel.

STOL
© 95

ADVICE TO THE FLEDGLING BC PILOT

This writer has flown in Baja for some thirty plus years. Although I have retired from flying, I still offer my advice to pilots planning a first penetration of the Baja California Peninsula. To wit:

1. Bring money!
2. Fly with the clean side of your aircraft up.
3. Bring Money!
4. Fly with the dirty side of your aircraft down.
5. Bring Money!
6. Fly with the pointy end of your aircraft forward.
7. Bring Money!
8. Keeping an ocean off each wing will solve navigational problems.
9. Bring Money!
10. If your fuel quantity gauge reads empty, you have reached your destination.
11. Bring Money!
12. If your oil pressure gauge reads "0", you have flown too far.
13. BRING MONEY!
14. Bring an ATM card in case your money plays out!

Remember

Gasoline on the ground is useless.
Altitude above you is useless.
A runway behind you is useless.
Your situation is grave when you run out of airspeed, altitude and ideas at the same time.
Keep 'em flying (WE NEED THE MONEY!)

FRANK FISCHER

Our scene is Santa Rosalía, Baja California, in the year 1914. Frank Fischer had arrived there in the capacity of a donkey engine-man on a German square rigged ship plying it's trade from Hamburg to the Baja California copper mines: coke from Europe for the furnaces and copper ingots on the back haul.

The war to end all wars broke out that year. A British cruiser was assigned to patrol the lower end of the Sea of Cortez and bottle up the ten German merchant ships in the Port of Santa Rosalía. The British message was loud and clear, "Gentleman, you are not military vessels and we are not at war with you. However, should you attempt to leave the Sea of Cortez, we will blow you out of the water!" The Germans were stuck in Santa Rosalía for the duration.

Santa Rosalía is not one of the garden spots on this planet. As time passed, some of the crewmen became a bit antsy and decided to try their luck and return to their homeland by other conveyance. Our hero, Frank, along with three companions hatched up a little scheme. They would walk across the peninsula to Scammon's Lagoon and board a whaler to return to their homeland. They walked fifty miles to San Ignacio where the natives advised them that to attempt a trek across the Viscaíno Desert was suicidal.

Frank's buddies decided to abandon the effort and return to Santa Rosalía. Frank's parting shot at the time he fled from ship had been to knock the first mate on the cranium with a pipe wrench and, as a result, he deemed it prudent to hang around San Ignacio rather than return to the punishment that awaited him on the square rigger.

Frank established camp in a remote palm grove below the San Ignacio Mission and began fabricating chairs. He was reluctant to show his face in the village because he was afraid the officers from his ship would be searching for him so he commissioned a certain Señorita Cruz Sandoval to sell his wares.

After a time, it became apparent that the ship officers had lost interest in Fischer and he came out of the palms and set up housekeeping with Señorita Cruz.

When the chair market became saturated, Frank became the village blacksmith.

Automobiles were introduced into Baja California in the 1920's and Frank was first a spring maker and later a mechanic. Overland American tourists began to appear in the 1950's and Frank Fischer's tri-lingual and mechanical abilities were much in demand. No guidebook was complete without a tribute to San Ignacio's fabled German mechanic.

One legend concerns a visiting American who asked, "Frank, I have heard that the Mexican boys make marvelous mechanics, is this true?"

"Come, let me show you." Frank escorted the gringo behind the shop and pointed to a broken anvil.

"But that's impossible!" said the pilgrim. "How did he break an anvil?"

"Persistence," Frank replied.

Frank and Cruz are long since dead. They left twelve offspring and an uncountable number of grandchildren and all the Fischer males are pretty good mechanics.

THE ETHICS OF PLUTARCO

One of the most sanctified pieces of ground in Baja California is located behind Mini Super Playas del Tesoro in Los Barriles. A two-foot-four-inch wall constructed of decorative blocks intended to protect Doña Lupe's ROSE GARDEN enshrines this hallowed ground. Save Plutarco, all beings are prohibited entry. Only Plutarco is cognizant of the tender loving care demanded by these very special roses, which require crooning and caressing while being watered, weeded or pruned, therefore he enjoys complete job security as our gardener one day each week. This condition had existed for several months when he informed Doña Lupe that, in his opinion, a salary adjustment was in order.

When Doña Lupe queried specifically what sort of an adjustment he had in mind he replied, "Doña Lupe, up to now, I've received my salary at the end of the working day, therefore I trust you for the entire day. I would like to receive my salary at mid-day. Thus it is demonstrated that I trust you throughout the morning, while you trust me for the afternoon."

Doña Lupe modified this plan somewhat. On alternate weeks Don Plutarco is paid at the beginning of the day. The remaining weeks his salary is paid at the end of the day.

GOD BLESS YOU MARIA

It came to pass that on September 7, 1984 tropical storm Marie was reported located at 18.4 degrees north by 109.2 degrees west with winds in excess of fifty-five knots. Her perimeter was 110 miles from center and her direction of travel was approximately three hundred twenty degrees. Torrents of rain fell on the cape of Baja California driven by winds that uprooted trees in Cabo San Lucas. Through superhuman efforts most of the fishing boats in San Lucas Bay were saved. Arroyos, normally dry, became raging cataracts and traffic came to a halt.

In La Ribera, however, *Chubasco Maria* will be discussed as a fond memory in years to come. It is reported that a fully laden truck carrying some two hundred fifty cases of that community's favorite brew attempted to negotiate the flooded dry wash on the northern edge of town. Success was in sight when the undermined bank the truck was crossing caved in and dumped the whole shebang *"patas por el cielo"* ("feet for the sky"). Thirty cases were rescued by the truck's valiant crew *"lo de mas se volo"* ("the rest, it flew"). Tecate drinkers, some in their Sunday best, waited at strategic points downstream from the mishap and intercepted the vagrant six-packs with heroic abandon akin to the berserkers of old.

Within an hour, all supplies of ice in the local stores had been depleted and the ammeter on the power plant indicated a sixty-percent increase in demand as overloaded refrigerators met the challenge.

It would be difficult to determine exactly how many beers this windfall supplied the individual consumer but obviously it was in excess. By mid afternoon, Tecate laden merrymakers were cruising the streets of La Ribera with ghetto blasters at maximum volume.

Ah, yes, a time to be remembered! However, negative words were uttered by certain elements of the populace. The above mentioned consignment of beer had been slated for sale at the dance scheduled on the night in question. Musicians playing at the dance work for a percentage of beer sales. The band arrived after no small amount of toil, considering the road condition, took a long lingering look at the situation, had a few beers and left town without off-loading their instruments.

The female populace, having been cheated out of their dance, was a bit miffed, as was the beer concessionaire who normally garners enough profit from these affairs to keep him in regal splendor.

All things considered, it is certain that if a poll were taken *Chubasco Maria* would win by a landslide.

A time to remember indeed!

GRAZIELLA'S BABY

Rancho Mesquital is located at the southern foot of the Tres Virgenes Volcanoes halfway between San Ignacio and Santa Rosalía. Flora "*La Muda*" ("Deaf-mute") Juárez was the grandam of this way stop for more years than anyone remembers. Flora's three claims to fame were: (1) she talked incessantly, (2) she had a memory like an elephant and served as the newspaper for the entire mid-peninsula, (3) she brewed the finest cup of coffee on the Camino Real (this was before it became Mexico Highway 1). A stop at Rancho Mesquital was a must for all passing travelers, local or trans-peninsular.

One often quoted statement by La Muda reflected on her report that a rainstorm had covered a vast territory: "From Tijuana to La Paz. All over the world." This told us much about the scope of Flora's world.

Another Flora history concerns Manuel Meza's gallstone operation. Manuel was returning to San Ignacio from surgery in Hermosillo when he stopped at Mesquital for the traditional cup of coffee. The conversation went something like this:

Flora: "Manuel, is it true they operated on you in Hermosillo?"

Manuel: "It is true, Flora. They removed stones from my *vesicula*."

Flora: "But Manuel, what do they look like?"

Manuel: "I have them in the car. Would you like to see them?"

Flora: "Oh, yes, please."

Manuel went outside the ranch house and picked up a couple of one pound rocks off the ground, put them in a paper bag and showed them to Flora.

"But, Manuel," she exclaimed, "how did you swallow them?"

Graziella, Flora's daughter, had a darling baby girl named Maristella. Maristella created a logistical problem at Rancho Mesquital. She demanded Carnation Condensed Milk in cans. Most of Flora's supplies arrived at the ranch via the twice-weekly mail truck. Chama, the driver of the mail truck, could supply Carnation Condensed Milk in the large cans only. This proved impractical because there was no refrigeration at Rancho Mesquital and about half of each can spoiled before use. The half-sized cans were available in a certain mercantile in Santa Rosalía but Chama refused to enter this store because of a tiff with the owner several years previous.

Your author usually flew down from San Ignacio to Santa Rosalía on Thursday mornings to purchase ham, cheese and bacon that had arrived on the ferry from Topolobampo during the previous night (the entire supply was sold before siesta time on Thursday but the shopkeeper refused to increase the order because his refrigerator would not hold a larger quantity). A week's supply of baby condensed milk was procured for Maristella and packaged tightly for an airdrop at Rancho Mesquital on the return trip. I would buzz the ranch; Graziella would come out and wave a towel and an airdrop into the corral would occur on the second pass. Some of the cans were dented on occasion but none ever ruptured. Graziella reimbursed me via the Friday mail.

Three years ago, I received a graduation announcement from the University of Guadalajara informing that Maristella was receiving a law degree with honors. Maristella is the Deputy District Attorney in Guerrero Negro now. Graziella? She's still at Rancho Mesquital, making coffee. I saw her there last month.

HEAD 'EM OFF AT THE GAS

The afternoon session at San José de Buena Vista Rural School begins at 1:00 P.M. Since the school is located on the west side of Mexico Highway 1 and most of the students live on the seaward side, speed bumps have been installed to slow traffic on the busy road. These speed bumps aren't always effective, therefore patrol car 007 can usually be seen parked in front of Las Gaviotas Restaurant around that time of day. The presence of this highly visible vehicle has a deterring effect on would-be speeders and requires practically no effort on the part of the attending policemen.

This state of affairs existed on a fine June afternoon last year when a new Volkswagen bearing mainland license plates made a hasty arrival.

"Compañeros," reported citizen Volkswagen driver, "I wish to report a drunk driver. He is driving a blue pickup truck and towing a large white boat on a trailer. If you hurry, you will catch him. He was southbound five minutes ago."

"Sr. Volkswagen driver," said the officer, "it is my sincere desire to help you with this problem but I have no gasoline in my patrol unit and my supervisors did not furnish me with funds to purchase same. An oversight, I'm sure."

Apparently, the blue pickup, towing a large white boat, reached its destination without incident. There was no report to the contrary.

HERO STORY

During the spring of 1980 floods in Northern Baja California played havoc with the roads. Tom Miller reported seven impassable breaks between San Quintín and the border.

Many private aircraft were pressed into service, moving relief goods south and stranded American tourists to the north.

A radio message from the Martinez family at Colonia Colonet reported that floodwaters had destroyed the food supply at their chili farm next to the river. Relatives in San Diego appealed for help.

It was necessary to land on the highway south of Colonia Colonet because the airstrip north of town was flooded and the bridge was out. "*Panzita Puerca*" ("Little Dirty Belly," so named for the ever-present oil streaks on her underside) and I off-loaded our cargo and departure was impending when a young lady approached me. She stated she was diabetic and had no medication. She wanted a lift back to San Diego. I took her aboard and we flew north.

Somewhere around Ensenada, my passenger reported that she felt very woozy and believed she was going into insulin shock. San Diego area radio was contacted and an emergency was declared. We were cleared for a straight-in approach to runway thirty-one at Lindbergh Field. When we arrived, a paramedic vehicle met us on the taxiway and a doctor administered medication immediately. Things were rosy, except: 1) we had not landed in Tijuana to clear customs and file a flight plan out of Mexico 2) I had not reported my impending arrival to US Customs one hour in advance 3) my passenger was not on my flight plan manifest 4) my passenger had no documentation to prove US citizenship.

US Immigration was inclined to cause a problem until the director received a phone call from my passenger's father (a prominent Los Angeles television executive.) That cleared us with INS.

US Customs decided that since I had declared an emergency, the one-hour advisory prior to arrival had not been violated, however, I had to return to Tijuana to square things with Mexican Customs and aeronautical authority.

At Tijuana, the Mexican officials were willing to forget and forgive, provided that I would fly south to El Rosario with another load of relief supplies. The aircraft was fueled, reloaded and we went south.

As we were off-loading on the highway at El Rosario (another flooded airstrip), I was informed that a radio call had reported a desperate need for an aircraft in Rancho Santa Inez.

We landed at Santa Inez as the sun disappeared over the Pacific. Single engine flight after dark is prohibited in Mexico and I had visions of more violations when I returned to Tijuana.

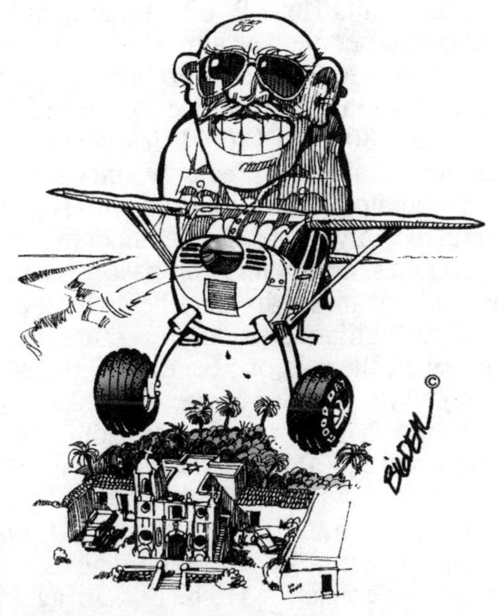

As we turned onto the parking apron at Santa Inez, a gringa ran across the apron waving her arms and screaming, "Thank God, you're here!"

"Yes, Ma'am," I replied, "I'm here. How can I help you?"

"I'm out of Pampers!" she tearfully replied, "CAN YOU BRING ME SOME PAMPERS?"

I'm out of the hero business now.

HIGHLANDERS

The people who live in the highland ranches of Baja California are of the old *Californio* stock. For the most part, the same families have inhabited these ranches for at least one hundred fifty years and in some instances two hundred twenty five. Many of the families in the cape region have English surnames: Collins, Richie, Green, Davis, Cunningham, McLish, Smith, Fisher, Robinson, Kennedy, and Sanders. All of these highland ranches were land grants to soldiers and missionary servants who served in the time of the Jesuits (l697-1767.) Land acquired by the foreign surnamed people was almost always, without fail, granted to sailors who jumped ship in one of the ports around the cape and married into one of the old land grant families between 1808 and 1860. Lifestyle in the highland ranches has not changed appreciably since missionary times. Battery-operated ghetto blasters and Tupperware seem to be about the only concessions to modern society. Fax machines, telephones, computers and passenger cars are regarded as aberrations in the divine scheme by the highlanders.

The highlanders seldom venture far from their ranches. However, there is one exception, the annual fiestas in the remote villages: San Javier, San José de Gracia, Comondú, Santiago, Miraflores, San Bartolo, Santa Gertrudis, San Borja and San Ignacio. The customs seem to be changing now, but slowly. Girls stay pretty close to the homestead until they had passed their fifteenth birthday. At *quinceañeras* (a fifteen year old girl's "coming out" party), they were considered to be of marriageable age and put on display.

The first order of business when these little *rancheras* arrived at the pueblo was to purchase their first pair of high-heeled shoes. One could always spot them at the promenade as they wobbled around the plaza at breakneck speed, giggling all the way. The shy ones would observe how the townies handled it for a few laps before joining in the fun. Their homemade ensembles were also somewhat notable except in the very remote villages where the townies were in the same boat.

When observing the promenade in back country villages during the *fiestas* around the cape region, the profusion of blue eyed blondes and green eyed red heads can be quite a startling experience. These young ladies are descendants from the old English surname families who have intermarried (cousins still marry frequently) for the last century and a half. While the custom of the *promenada* was abandoned in the city, it is alive and well in the small pueblo. Young ladies parade around the plaza in-groups of two to four under the watchful eyes of their *dueñas* (chaperones) who usually occupy the park benches. Interested males pretend to be engaged in profound conversation on the outer perimeter while ogling the parade.

When the time is right, the males form small groups and stroll around the plaza in the opposite direction. Those in the final phases of *cortejo* (courtship) stroll at a leisurely pace holding hands. This method of merchandising has been around since plazas were invented. Perhaps plazas came into existence for this express purpose.

The male members of the highland families have attended school in the *pueblos* during the last fifty years while boarding with relatives or living in *enternados* (boarding facilities operated by the Secretariat of Education). Many of these youngsters abandon the ranch life after being seduced by the sophistication of the villages. Production on these ranches is small and therefore will support a limited number of people, making the abandonment desirable. However, it is entirely possible that this migration will result in vacated ranches after the older generation dies off.

Many rural roads have been constructed during the last decade. Isolated ranches and villages who had historically never seen a motor vehicle are accessible now. San Francisco de la Sierra was a hard three-day mule trip from San Ignacio some twenty years past and is now visited almost daily by tourists who come to view the cave paintings. Ignorant tourists will naturally conclude that the simple life of the people of San Francisco is deficient and introduce TV, cellular phones and designer jeans. It will be a great loss.

HIPOLITO

Hipolito Arce was a one hundred ten-pound chunk of rawhide with one blue eye that sighted his audience with a penetration that created the sensation that he had the facility of peering into one's soul. The other eye, of a nondescript color, sort of wandered out toward Jones' barn. Hipolito was unmarried and resided in the Sierra San Francisco. He was related to all the families inhabiting the remote ranches of the sierra and seemed to have no permanent base. While Hipolito was a master at all crafts essential to survival in "them thar hills," his principal source of income seemed to be mule packing. He would appear in San Ignacio four or five times a year, his beasts loaded with white cheese, jerky, fire wood, tanned cow hides and, last but not least, arrowheads. The arrowheads were traded to your reporter for tequila and were utilized to work nefarious scams on passing gringos (but that's another story). After boozing it up in San Ignacio for a few days, he returned to the mountains with his train loaded with store bought goods for the ranches.

It must have been about thirty five years ago that a gringa spinster appeared in San Ignacio with a singular need. She was on of those folks who tack letters like MA, Ph.D and such after their name and expect us less fortunates to call them "Doctor".

It seems that the doctor wished to travel the out-backs of the Sierra San Francisco to confirm the existence of a certain species of ground squirrel. The doctor was ignorant of the local idiom, so that's where I come in.

Hipolito was summoned from the hills to serve as outfitter and negotiation transpired. Hipolito would supply six mules. One mule for the doctor, one mule for the guide/ interpreter (me), one mule for Hipolito (mule packer) and one mule for one of Hipolito's nieces who was to serve as camp cook as well as the guardian of the doctor's virtue. The remaining beasts would transport the camp. I was most curious as Hipolito charged forty dollars each for the mules that were to be ridden, while the remaining four mules would serve for a week for only ten dollars each. What the hell! The doctor was on a grant and Hipolito needed the money.

After a week in the high country the great chipmunk expedition returned to civilization with two live specimens of the elusive antelope ground squirrel and numerous photos of the now famous cave paintings. We arrived in San Ignacio late in the evening and the doctor and I were dropped at Casa Leree the local *pension* (boarding house) with the understanding that we would contact Hipolito at a relative's house to settle accounts on the following morning.

The discrepancy on the price of the mules became apparent when we paid our bill. After the agreed amount had been paid, the doctor and I were taking our leave when Hipolito queried, "What's wrong with the mules?"

"Nothing," I replied, "a little tired from the trip but nothing a couple of days rest won't cure."

"Then why aren't you taking them with you?"

"Because they are your mules, Hipolito."

"But you paid me fair and square for the mules, market value!"

"No, Hipolito, I only rented those mules."

It is most interesting to note that a local guide quoted fifty dollars a day rent per mule to take a party into the Sierra de la Laguna here in Los Barriles last week.

There is something wrong in an economy when a mule earns five times as much as our gardener.

THE KUDU

The late Nate Dubin was a medical doctor. When not engaged in the healing profession, Nate loved to fish in the Sea of Cortez or hunt big game in Africa. Nate was the answer to a taxidermist's prayer. After some forty years, Nate's collection of large mounted fish and animal heads was crowding him out of house and office. Helen (Mrs. D) rebelled and Nate was forced to seek other residences for some of the mounts. The kudu (*Tragelaplus strepsiceros*) now hangs over the fireplace in the bar at Hotel Palmas de Cortez.

The decor in the aforementioned bar is definitely nautical. Fifty-two mounted marine species from the waters of the East Cape surrounding a kudu head make it stand out like a petunia in an onion patch.

Pilgrims arriving from the land of K-Mart go for their courtesy margarita as soon as they have donned the uniform of the day. They nibble at their margarita, they ogle the decor and they make inquiry as to how in hell did a kudu wind up in a Baja California bar?

Hector, the resident barkeep at this hour, has tried to deal with this question innumerable times. After reading disappointment in a thousand pilgrim faces when told the truth, he now retreats behind the language barrier.

Bob Hoagland, spotted as a local by a rather astute pilgrim, rose to the occasion:

Pilgrim, "You live around here?"

Hoagland, "Yep."

Pilgrim, "What kind of a head is that?"

Hoagland, "Kudu."

Pilgrim, "But, there are no kudus in Baja."

Hoagland, "There are now."

Pilgrim, "How did they get here?"

Hoagland, "A guy brought in some breeding stock from Africa and turned them loose down behind Punta Colorada. They're doin' fine."

Pilgrim, "Why did he do that?"

Hoagland, "He charges people to hunt them."

Pilgrim, "You mean to tell me I could shoot a kudu right near here."

Hoagland, "Yep, but it's expensive."

Pilgrim, "How much?"

Hoagland, "Five thousand dollars a shot, hit or miss!"

Pilgrim, "Where do I find this guy?

Hoagland, "Oh, he'll be along after a bit, comes in every night. Hector'll point him out to you. His name is Jim Smith."

When I wandered into Palmas Bar some two hours later, I was met by a man with glazed eyes, wearing a pith helmet and brandishing a check for five thousand dollars. He wanted to go on safari to the jungles of Punta Colorada at six o'clock on the following morning.

Bob and Chacha Van Wormer told Hoagland not to work that scam again. Seems the pilgrim was truly miffed at missing his kudu and said he would not patronize their hotel again!

IGNACIO ROJAS' LOST SILVER MINE

Lost Jesuit mission treasure legends abound in Baja California. Nights around the campfire with local people are incomplete without some tale concerning a misplaced fortune in silver, pearls or gold. The most often-told goes something like this:

The Jesuits in Spain learned about Carlos III's impending expulsion order shortly after it was formulated. Jesuit thumping had become a pastime in the royal houses of Europe and Mexican Jesuits had rightly anticipated an expulsion and confiscation of their treasure. A secret mission was constructed in a remote place and the Baja California Jesuit treasure was concealed therein.

Local theory has it that news of the expulsion was received calmly by the resident fathers since they had been anticipating this news for some time. Names of these lost missions vary with the individual yarn-spinner. The most popular are Santa Isabel, Santa Clara and Santa Magdalena.

In 1759, the year Carlos III ascended to the throne of Spain, the Chief Minister of Portugal had successfully uprooted the entire Jesuit organization in that country and confiscated the order's wealth for the crown. France was involved in a long court proceeding that was leading toward the end of Jesuit influence in that country. An expulsion order was exercised in New Spain (Mexico) and arrests were made on June 25, 1767, but the envoy did not arrive in San Bernabe (near San José del Cabo) until November 30, 1767. Harry Crosby in his epic Jesuit history, *Antigua California*, relates that when the envoy, Gaspar de Partolo, brought the news to padre Ignacio Tirsh at San José del Cabo, it was received with calm resignation, leading one to believe the Jesuits might have had some forewarning of the impending expulsion.

While modern scholars deny these lost mission stories, popular writers have a ball with them. My yarn does not have to do with a lost mission but a lost vein of silver near the beach some thirty-seven miles south of Loreto. This lost silver mine is documented in the Clemente Gullen Diaries of 1719-1721 (#42 in the *Dawson Travel Series* as translated by Michael W. Mathis Ph.D):

"Friday the 15th (1720). We entered San Carlos Aripaquí. Having traveled about five leagues, the two summits of Acuré and Aripaquí were traversed with great difficulty with the cargo. Many of the pack mules fell and rolled over, and in some cases with great risk of killing the mules. Other loads came unpacked, and thus we were delayed on the trail. It was very laborious crossing these summits. On a hill near San Carlos Aripaquí, Corporal Ignacio de Rojas found a good vein of silver. We were well received by the people of Aripaquí, and two of them accompanied us, serving well to introduce us in the subsequent rancherías. A shallow well was dug for the horses and mules, and about two leagues were explored.

Saturday the 16th. We went to San Gregorio Asembavichí. This would be about three leagues of good trail. Along the trail we found a slough surrounded by saline deposits which are very necessary for the manufacture of soap. Here it was hard work to dig a shallow well so that the horses and mules could drink. In this wash we found grinding stones that were very good and of all sizes. Today about three leagues ahead were explored."

To give creditability to Rojas as a prospector, we have this passage from *Antiqua California,* "a soldier, Ignacio Rojas, had discovered silver at Santa Ana in 1720. Padre Ignacio María Nápoli was in the process of establishing a mission there when on of the structures collapsed in a storm, killing a number of neophytes. The Indians construed this to be a plot and forced padre Nápoli to flee for his life. The project was abandoned."

If Padre Nápoli's objective was saving souls rather than mining silver, Santa Ana seems a rather curious site to found a mission. You can bet your bippie that while not recorded, Ignacio Rojas was the resident soldier (i.e. mine developer) with Padre Nápoli when this little caper went down.

The Santa Ana mining region, including San Antonio, El Triunfo, Gallenas, Tescalama and Trinchero, has been exploited since 1748. As this is written, a Canadian company is working the old Trinchero diggin's some two hundred eighty years after Rojas' discovery.

Going to look for it? I'll supply you a map for a fee!

SAUDI ARABIAN TAMALES

One of the greatest logistical triumphs ever perpetrated by "can-do" Yankee ex-patriots in Jeddah, Saudi Arabia, was initiated one winter morning in 1978 when your author casually remarked, "My wife makes wonderful tamales."

This chance remark was received with great enthusiasm in the executive offices of Dallah/Avco Ltd. This company is responsible for all airport maintenance in the Kingdom of Saudi Arabia and yours truly was summarily dispatched to consult Doña Lupe and compile a list of needed supplies, which read something like this:

1. A twenty-gallon pot with lid for steaming tamales.
2. A suitable grate to fit the above listed pot (tamales are steamed about four inches above water in the pot).
3. Fifty pounds of *masa harina* (corn flour).
4. Four hundred corn shucks to wrap the tamales.
5. Ten pounds of New Mexico red chilies (preferably from Gallenas Valley).
6. Fifteen pounds of lean pork (strictly prohibited by Muslim law).
7. Twenty chickens.

A survey was conducted and revealed that the only items on the list available locally were the pot, the lid and the chickens, which made it clear that a certain amount of smuggling would be necessary, particularly in the instance of the pork. Since this was to be expedited by pilots and/or aircrews flying international routes, these co-conspirators had to be included in the guest list for the *tamalada* (tamale feast).

Assignments went out and the order was filled in less than two weeks in the following manner:

Item 1. The grate was fabricated of stainless steel in the sheet metal repair sections of Saudi Airlines.

Item 2. *Masa harina* was procured in a Cincinnati super market by the aircrew in Sheik Sala Camel's personal Boeing 707 while on standby in that city.

Item 3. Corn shucks were procured in Oklahoma City

by a TWA Boeing 747 crew while on standby and transferred to another TWA 747 crew in Boston who passed them to a Saudi Airlines L 10-ll in London.

Item 4. New Mexico red chilies were obtained when Sheik Sala's 707 made a special landing (costing some four-hundred dollars) in Albuquerque while en-route to Disneyland with the Sheik's wives and progeny aboard.

Item 5. Captain Bill Sapp supplied the pork in the company Hawker Siddley 125-600 from Frankfurt.

On landing at Jeddah Airport, the contraband was transferred to a fire-fighting vehicle, which departed the airport with siren and red emergency lights functioning. This emergency vehicle proceeded directly to the Smith villa and was rendered inoperative as soon as it left the airport.

Fatma, the Pakistani housemaid, assisted Doña Lupe. Some three days of intense labor produced three hundred-fifty fat Baja California-style tamales. An identifying red thread was tied to the pork tamales to avoid dispatching our Arab friends into eternal hell.

Some seventy guests, including Dallah/AVCO executives, international aircrews, Jeddah airport firefighters, Saudi Airlines sheet metal mechanics and a smattering of Arab friends attended the first, and perhaps only, Jeddah *tamalada* at the Smith villa that evening.

After the first serving had been accomplished, a catch-as-catch-can self-service riot was initiated on the tamale pot.

Abdulazis Camel, Dallah/AVCO's director of project control, was overheard advising an unidentified Arab companion, "Grab the tamales with the red thread, they're tastier!"

Casa Leree was sort of a boarding house that covered about one quarter of a block on Morales Street in San Ignacio. It was of the traditional adobe with a palm thatched roof structure surrounding the perimeter of the property. The large inside patio was covered by a grapevine arbor over a hundred years old. A rock-lined *acequia* (irrigation ditch), dating back to missionary times, meandered across the patio creating a most pleasant atmosphere. Doña Maria and Doña Chala Leree, daughters of Francisco Leree a French mining engineer who worked in the old French copper mines and smelters in Santa Rosalía, operated the *pension* in the old family home. Doña Maria was widowed. Doña Chala never married.

Doña Maria's daughter, Rebecca, had moved to Los Angeles, married and raised a family. She worked as a bilingual secretary in the movie studios around Hollywood after Mr. Carillo, her artist husband, died. When Doña Maria was about eighty years old she became blind. The boarding house and Doña Maria became more than the seventy-five year old Chala could handle alone, so Beca returned to Casa Leree to assist.

Beca Carillo's linguistic abilities soon made Casa Leree a favorite stopping place for all gringos passing through. This, coupled with the residual Mexican clientele, soon became more than Beca and Chala could cope with so they elected to bring in some help. Chuey (*"La Piernuda"* or "Leggy One") Arce was brought in from Rancho San Luis, a remote cattle ranch.

Strapping Chuey, of a very sunny disposition and much energy, had spent her entire life on the ranch in company of her immediate family. Her older sisters had married leaving only her parents and four bachelor brothers. Chuey was most anxious to please as she was very happy in San Ignacio and only wished to return to Rancho San Luis for very short visits. Her constant companion was a battery powered portable radio, which was always operated at maximum volume. And Chuey danced, a *comba* while sweeping, a *corrido* while mopping, a *cha cha cha* while washing dishes, a waltz while hanging clothes and, most spectacular of all, a rumba while at the cook stove. She loved the morning! She arose at 5:00 A.M. with the afterburner in full power. She shined, she glistened, she radiated, and she danced, accompanied by that infernal radio (a gift from yours truly).

What must be understood is that I regard rising earlier than 9:00 A.M. an abortion in the divine scheme. Mornings are very horrid and private. Oh, how I dreaded those arrivals at the kitchen for that first cup of coffee to be overwhelmed by Chuey's morning brilliance.

"Buenos días, señor!"

I always replied, "Buenos goddamn días, Chuey."

I vacated the digs at Casa Leree for a little sojourn in Southeast Asia to slay dragons, save the world for democracy and, coincidentally, pick up a few bucks. My chief concern was Chuey's welfare during my absence. This problem resolved itself with the arrival of Jerry and Eloise Klink. They had come down from El Cajon to spend a few months at Casa Leree and thereby assured Chuey's employment.

Jerry was a kindred sole and greeted the new day with an enthusiasm equal to my own, except perhaps an hour later. He swore that on his first morning in residence, Chuey appeared at his bedside at 5:30 A.M., bearing two steaming cups of coffee and a grin that would eat a banana sideways. She announced, "BUENOS GODDAMN DÍAS, PATRON!"

THE KISSING CAPTAIN

Pancho Muñoz, the gallant owner, operator, chief pilot and public relation's manager of the now-defunct Baja Airlines, had a singular habit. He kissed all his female passengers as they boarded and deplaned. They loved it!

Francisco (Pancho) Muñoz first flew solo in a Curtis Junior Pusher on February 7, 1937, at Ciudad Chihuahua, two months short of his eighteenth birthday. After receiving his private license, he flew sightseeing passengers for two years and acquired the necessary two hundred hours of flying time to apply for his commercial pilot's license. While the ink was drying on the newly acquired certificate, our hero pulled stakes and left for Mexico City to apply for a pilot's seat with Aeronaves de Mexico. After a short interview, the station manager marched Pancho down to the parking area and showed him a Stinson Detroiter and announced that the plane should be at work in Oaxaca on the following day. Pancho admitted he had not flown a Stinson Detroiter and asked if someone could "check him out" on it. The station manager stated, "Hell, you're a pilot aren't you? Check yourself out en route to Oaxaca." Muñoz immediately set out to buy a map so he could find out where Oaxaca was located.

Departure for Oaxaca was cut short when excessive engine vibration was noted. Pancho returned to the maintenance hanger and reported the problem to the chief mechanic who asked, "Ever flown a radial engine before?"

Pancho admitted he had no radial engine experience, to which the mechanic replied,

"Well, they vibrate!" as he walked away.

His honor on the line, Pancho departed with a heavy load of spare parts aboard and spent a sweaty thirty minutes circling the valley of Mexico to gain altitude to get over the mountains. As Tehuacan was approached, the pilot was thoroughly convinced that something was wrong and landed. He dispatched a telegram to Mexico City for mechanical assistance.

The chief mechanic arrived in a disgruntled state after an all night train ride and reluctantly agreed to check the propeller. One blade was four inches shorter than the other.

The mechanic produced a hacksaw and was preparing to prune the excess when Muñoz suggested that perhaps they should install the extra propeller, which was in cargo. Inspection revealed that the spare prop also had a blade that was shy four inches. The blades had been transposed during a recent overhaul. A blade change soon had the Detroiter purring like a kitten and en route to Oaxaca.

Muñoz's circuit in Oaxaca started at the capital city six days a week laden with passengers and mail. The route was between tiny hamlets, which were never separated by more than ten minutes flying time. No roads connected these villages and their dirt landing strips seldom exceeded six hundred meters in length. Survival was testimony to the pilot's ability.

1942 offered Muñoz an opportunity to work for the US government expanding Mexico's airstrips to accommodate the American warplanes.

As WWII wound down, Pancho took a job flying a DC-3 for a Yucatan lumber company, hauling executives and doing aerial surveys to locate mahogany forests in bloom. The lumber company fell into political disfavor and was dissolved, which forced Muñoz to move to Texas where he sold Piper Airplanes.

While on a business trip to San Diego, Pancho struck up a conversation with Jim Bracamonte at Lindberg field and learned that Tijuana had no air service. This knowledge inspired Pancho to create Baja Airlines, which was a real shoestring operation in 1955 with only one four-place Cessna 170. Business was slow and our "Kissing Captain" supplemented his income by flying old Douglas B-18s to the remote Baja California lobster fishing camps on the Pacific, between El Rosario and San Juanico. His manifest on the southbound leg of these flights would be supplies for the camps. The northbound leg was six thousand pounds of live lobster in wet gunnysacks.

The application to upgrade the operation from a charter service to a scheduled airline was being ground through the wheels of bureaucracy when our legendary captain had the good fortune to be summoned for a flight from Guerrero Negro to Tijuana, by no other than Erle Staley Gardner, author of the fabled Perry Mason series. The pilot and the writer were soon fast friends. As the relation blossomed,

Muñoz became one of the chief characters in Gardener's four subsequent books concerning his exploration of the peninsula. The resulting publicity generated by these books soon had Baja Airline's flying with a route permit to Bahía de Los Angeles, Mulegé and Guerrero Negro (many residents here on the peninsula suspected the famous author was an investor in this airline).

Quoting from *Air Progress Magazine,* July 1967: "Captain Muñoz now has thirty-four employees. Baja Airlines has a forty passenger Martin 202, two eighteen passenger Lockheed Loadstars, a Beechcraft C-45 and a Cessna 195. At this same time, more than sixty-five percent of his landings are still on dirt strips. Muñoz commanded uncanny ability to bring his planes to a safe stop on the shortest of landing strips. This writer watched, goggle-eyed, as Muñoz brought in a fully (and I mean fully) loaded Beechcraft into a downhill dirt strip just 1,350 feet long. There were gullies at both ends and absolutely no room for error. Francisco Muñoz touched down "three point" in exactly the same spot on successive flights within thirty feet of the beginning of the runway and coasted to a stop with minimum breaking. Captain Muñoz, for our money, is the best short field pilot we've ever seen in action."

1970 was a bleak year for our Captain. His pal, Erle Stanley Gardner, died and the publicity dried up. Aeronaves de Mexico decided to expand their operations into Baja California since it was a proven moneymaker. Muñoz fought this in court but the judge ruled that Aeronaves was a federally owned airline and the routes belonged to them. Baja Airlines' permits were revoked and Muñoz was out of business.

Pancho Muñoz became chief pilot for Exportadora de Sal (the salt company in Guerrero Negro). He retired from that job at the age of sixty-five in 1983. His logbook shows 23,239 hours and 25 minutes but he admitted it had been shaved because he could only log ninety hours per month to be legal.

Captain Franciso Muñoz, license #237, will be long remembered in Baja, especially by those he kissed as they boarded a flight to Mulegé or Bahía de Los Angeles.

LAS VIRGENES (The Virgins)

During Jesuit times (1697-1767) the trans-peninsular road was nothing more than a trail marked by an occasional Latin cross chipped into trailside rocks. Those crosses were commonly referred to as *Las Virgenes* and served a dual purpose. They were a commercial break for the Virgin Mary as well as being road signs. Many travelers would pay homage at the shrine before continuing their journey and frequently camped for the night at the site. This route was called *El Camino Real*, usually translated as The Kings Highway. Some scholars believe that this is a poor translation since, in most dictionaries, the word *real* translates into true or real, making the trail the true highway indicating that the traveler is not lost.

When automobile traffic was initiated in the 1920s the original route was altered from *El Camino Real* due to terrain too rough for cars but the name remained. The virgins on this rustic road soon evolved from simple crosses etched in rock into roadside shrines wherein candles were frequently left burning by passing travelers. At a shrine near Cataviña a hibiscus thrived on water supplied by passing motorists.

When President Luis Echeverria Álvarez inaugurated the paved highway in 1973, *El Camino Real* became Mexico Highway 1 and new *Virgenes* soon appeared. While many of these *Virgenes* were intended for their original purpose, others marked the scene of a traffic fatality.

The rediscovery of an ancient shrine has caused a bit of a sensation lately. This monument is located in the arroyo of Las Canoas about four miles from the old ship landing at Surcadero de Cerralvo. Traditions passed down through the old families living in the area lead your reporter to believe that this shrine was indeed created in 1763 (as chiseled into the rock), probably by mule drivers as they waited for a ship to arrive with supplies for the mines at San Antonio and Santa Ana.

LAS BOMBAS MUNICIPAL AIRPORT

The base of my desk was originally intended to support a Singer sewing machine. The windshield of a defunct Volkswagen served for a desktop. On this makeshift desk was situated my old Underwood Standard typewriter. This whole arrangement was in exile in a shady corner of the grape arbor covering Doña Maria Leree's patio in San Ignacio. I was placidly bashing my cranium against the great American novel situated in Baja California when my Godfather, Tavo Villa arrived.

"Godson, what is it that you are doing?"

"Definitely, nothing productive," I replied.

"Then, perhaps you can help me with my problem."

"Indeed? Let's hear it."

"Well, Godson, it comes to pass that Alfredo owes me some money and I learned that he did very well in a poker game in Las Bombas last night."

"And?"

"Well, Godson, I think that if I could catch him while the glow is still on, I just might collect what is due me."

"So?"

"As you well know, Godson, it is some six hours driving to Las Bombas but you can cover this distance in less than an hour in your flying machine." (Highway 1 did not exist in those days.)

"This is true, Godfather, but you are overlooking one detail. There is no airport at Las Bombas."

"Then perhaps we could land at the airport in Guerrero Negro. After all, it is only eleven kilometers from Alfredo's establishment in Las Bombas. I could take a taxi from there."

Here, we must insert the fact the Las Bombas (The Pumps) is the red light district serving Guerrero Negro. There are five houses of joy located, completely alone, in one of the most forlorn stretches of the fabled Viscaíno Desert. As is recalled, two of these houses are situated on the west side of the main (and only) street, while three establishments are on the east side. Alfredo was the proprietor of the middle house on the east side of the one-hundred-foot wide main street.

OFICINA

We were inbound for Guerrero Negro, over Las Bombas, when Tavo reported, "Look, Godson. Alfredo's pickup is parked in front of his whorehouse. What a damned shame that we can't land there on the road and catch the bastard."

"Well," sez I, "the wind is right. Want to try it?"

"Your mother wears combat boots if we don't!"

"Tighten your seat belt, Godfather!"

Our landing on the main street of Las Bombas was textbook perfect! We rolled out routinely and taxied into a position blocking Alfredo's pickup.

We deplaned, entered and caught Alfredo having breakfast. Tavo collared him and since this was none of my affair, I chose to have coffee with one of the hostesses some distance from the pow-wow. The constabulary entered.

"There is an airplane parked outside!" reported the policeman.

"This is true," I admitted.

"This cannot be," he stated. "This is not an airport."

While I was casting about for an appropriate retort to this statement, my godfather entered from the rear. "*Compañero*, are you cognizant of whom you are addressing?" Tavo fixed the *chota* with a baleful stare.

"Well, no," admitted the cop.

"Come, we need to talk."

Tavo and the policeman went into a secluded corner and had a rather long conversation in low tones. The policeman returned to where the hostess and I sat and mumbled something about being pardoned for molesting me and took his leave.

Tavo collected his money and we returned to the aircraft to discover the policeman was holding traffic to assure us a safe takeoff.

"Tavo, what did you tell that cop?"

"James, my boy, you are now the only gringo general in the Mexican Air Force."

"And he believed that?"

"Sure! Who, but a general, would land an airplane at a whorehouse?

He had a point!

MACHISMO

Machismo is the stuff the Mexican male gets with his mother's milk! Poor guy, he doesn't have a chance. Mom lays it on thick from the day he's born. "I'm looking out for you now and when you're grown and your old man leaves me for a younger woman (or women) I'm calling in my bets and expect you to haul the freight for dear old doting mommy." The advertising media capitalizes on this for some two months prior to Mothers Day implying that if dear old mom is awarded anything less than a new Mercedes she has born a cheapskate.

The human male encounters a crossroads about the time he reaches puberty. Maternal influences are possibly the single greatest factor deciding whether our subject turns right or left. A guy who has been swinging on mom's tit for about 12 years discovers he has a tendency to make the wrong turn and become the ultimate Mexican disgrace: the *puto* (homosexual). Motivated by peer pressure primarily, this dude rebels against this discovery with every fiber in his being. He demonstrates his *machoismo* in numerous and sundry ways: aggressive driving, opening his shirt to the third button and wearing a huge medallion, drinking excessively, and pursing females with a vengeance.

Firearms and motor vehicles are the most notable extensions on the Mexican phallus. Weddings and New Years Eve parties are frequently climaxed by some drunk (usually a soft-clothed cop) haulin' out the ole hawg leg and blowing a few holes in the sky (on one remembered occasion, the casualty was a barroom chandelier). The epitome of *macho* exhibitionism is achieved with large diesel trucks. First off, all large diesel tractors are equipped with a gate which routes escaping exhaust gasses into an open pipe rather than the muffler, resulting in a resounding din. The felony is compounded by an apparatus called the "jake brake", which is designed to slow the vehicle with the drag of a dead engine. When applied, the jake brake produces a retort rivaling a .50 caliber anti-aircraft gun. When a female (or any other audience for that matter) is discovered by Mr. Macho the jake brake is brought into play, one of the most curious forms of masturbation known.

Another formidable apparatus in the *machismo* weaponry is the ghetto blaster. Numerous and sundry *pesos* are expended on state-of-the-art stereophonic sound reproduction systems. These reproduction systems are most frequently installed in little Japanese pick-ups in order to accommodate the huge speakers, which are carried in the truck beds. Evenings and Sundays are spent operating this equipment at maximum volume while cruising; treating the public to concerts of newly arrived Mexican rap or snail oompah bands with a smattering of Vincente Fernandez's latest hits. It would never enter Mr. Macho's head that other people who are engaged in conversation, watching television, or rocking the baby to sleep might be offended.

A variation on the old juvenile game of "chicken" involves dimming headlights for oncoming traffic. He who dims lights first is chicken thus creating the need for road signs stating *Conceda Cambio de Luces* (Dim Your Headlights).

Credit cards are flashed on the slightest provocation within the *macho* peer group. American Express capitalizes on this with the below-described television commercial. The scene opens with a handsome couple (she is sexy, blue eyed and practically bare) in a very expensive restaurant. The waiter presents the check, which is covered very ceremoniously by an AMEX card. The announcer comes on with *"Con el poder de su firma"* ("With the potency of your signature").

The *macho* attitude toward the fair sex is practically impossible to understand. Illegitimate offspring are an accepted proof that an individual is very *macho* indeed. However our subject seems to feel no concern for his illegitimate children or for the mother. *Machos* demand fidelity of their wives, while feeling no responsibility to respond in kind. A graphic demonstration of affluence is the big house/little house system. Maintaining a legitimate family residence with a kept mistress in a love nest is proof of sexual potency as well as proof of wealth. The legitimate matriarch in this situation responds classically by pampering the male offspring. "I'm looking out for you now and when you grow up I'm going to call in my markers."

A natural product of the *machismo* syndrome is the "junior," AKA *"niño bien"*. This appalling creature has been hanging around in the Latin culture for quiet a spell now. According to James A. Mitchner, he was formerly known as the *"hidalgo* or *"hijo de algo"* ("son of someone important"). He draws this status as if it were a pistol. When reproached, particularly by traffic cops, his first remark is, "Do you know who my father is?" Regrettably, this tactic is usually effective.

Junior surrounds himself with hangers-on who bask in the glory of his status. These pathetic individuals are constantly reminded that their membership in the gang is at the pleasure of Junior and in jeopardy. This undoubtedly accounts for the alarming number of "yes" men in Mexico.

Junior's favorite toy is a four wheel drive pickup equipped with oversized off-road tires, racing paint scheme, roll bars, decals and oftentimes a racing number copied in style of SCORE competitors in the Baja California off road-races. He has been known to don a dirty driver's uniform and cruise downtown La Paz for several days after the race has ended in an effort to create the illusion that he competed. Save Junior's entourage, no one is impressed.

The below listed song has been a Mexican cantina favorite for about a century.

El Abandonado

Me abandonaste mujer por que soy muy pobre
y por tener la desgracia de ser casado
que voy hacer si yo soy el abandonado
abandonado sea por el amor de dios.
Tres vicios tengo y los tengo muy arrasisado
de ser borracho judado y enamorado
que voy hacer si yo soy el abandonado
abandonado sea por el amor de dios.

The Abandoned One

You left woman, because I am very poor
and because of the disgrace that I am married
What shall I do if I am the abandoned one
Abandoned one for the love of God
Three vices have I and I have them deeply rooted
To be drunk, a playboy and in love.
What shall I do if I am the abandoned one?
Abandoned for the love of God.

No evening passes in a cantina without at least four requests for this little ditty

QUE PIENSA!
¿SE VENDE AQUI.. TACOS?
TACOS

MANGOS ENLATADA

Something in the neighborhood of forty-five years have past since Mr. Gonzales decided he could make a killing with a mango cannery in San José del Cabo. Mangos were cheap. Labor was cheap. It was not feasible to ship them fresh by truck because no road existed. Mr. Gonzales concluded about the only way to get his product to market would be *enlatada* (canned).

While work in his installation was in progress, Mr. Gonzales became sensitive to his potential market. He haunted grocery stores and observed that foreign tourists were buying an inordinate amount of canned fruit. He decided to shoot for the tourist market and print one side of the label on the cans in English. The dictionary was consulted and the result was predictable - mango=handle. The Spanish side of the label read: "*Mangos enlatada en su propio jugo*", while the English side read: "Handles canned in his own juice."

They sold like hotcakes! Visiting Americans bought "*Mangos enlatada*" by the case but for the wrong reason. They were taking them home as curios. Mr. Gonzales was advised that he had used improper English on his product. He changed the label and killed the goose.

MEXICANEERING

Solutions to mechanical problems faced by the backcountry Baja Califlornio are oftentimes unique and imaginative. Parts for repair and economic resources are often not available, thus motivating repairs with whatever material is at hand. An Evinrude outboard motor at Isla San José was observed operating rather efficiently with a cylinder head secured with sinew from the hind leg of a deer. The securing bolts were absent. Alignment was achieved by driving wooden dowels into the boltholes and fresh sinew was wrapped around the base and the cylinder head. The sinew shrank as it dried and supplied the needed torque.

Juan Lopez of El Arco frequently repaired damaged radiators by opening the damaged tubes and filling them with cotton. After the cotton was inserted, the tube was squeezed closed with pliers.

Auto tires became very scarce in the US during WW II. In Baja California, tires were totally unavailable. An ingenious owner of a Model A Ford in Santa Rosalía solved this problem by wrapping green rawhide around the bare rims. The rawhide shrank as it dried and became firm. The car was still operating on the rawhide tires in 1953.

A standard procedure for starting trucks with dead batteries on the outlying ranches was (and still is) to jack up a rear wheel, wrap a *riata* (rope) around the lifted wheel and pull the *riata* to start rotation.

Don Vidal Ceseña of San Ignacio drove a 1928 Ford Model A truck that had been retired from the US Postal Service until around 1969. The rear tires featured "boots" cut from other tires. Carriage bolts secured these "boots". The half dome heads of the bolts were installed inside the tire thus causing no damage to the inner tube. These tires remained in service for over fifteen years.

José Rosas Villavicencio of Rancho El Barril used an old 1935 Dodge truck more years than anyone remembers. The radiator became hors de combat and was replaced with a fifty-five gallon drum. A faucet was installed at the bottom of the drum. Seven daughters, bearing buckets, met the arriving truck in the evening. The hot water was transferred from the "radiator" drum to another drum atop the shower house and hot showers were a luxury enjoyed by all.

My buddy, Mike Warner, had a tire repaired in the village of Jesús Maria. The *llantero* used strips of old inner tube saturated with glue and pushed them into a tubeless tire with a screwdriver. Mike swears he arrived at Napa, California (about fifteen hundred miles) without loosing an ounce of air.

Art Willis became a Baja California legend by recovering broken or bent American aircraft for insurance companies. He was called to repair and ferry a skinned up Cessna from Rancho Timbabichi, south of Loreto. On arrival, he discovered the rancher had converted the nose gear into a wheelbarrow. Art had to fly to La Paz and buy a replacement wheelbarrow before the rancher would return the nose gear.

PELONA THE COW

The lowland Baja California rancher's attitude toward livestock is totally beyond gringo comprehension (the highland ranchers continue to live in the mountains as in the days of yore, and should not be included in this discussion). Open range laws have existed for close to three centuries now and old habits die hard. Under open range law, the owner of an animal has no responsibility for damages perpetrated by his wandering livestock. When berated concerning damages caused by his trespassing animals, the owner has a stock answer. "You should build a better fence!"

Since missionary times the BC rancher has been a parasite on cattle as much as a tick or a flea. His total livelihood is dependent on the bovine. This is an ideal arrangement because animal husbandry as practiced by lowland BC ranchers requires very little physical effort. Water is scarce and since cattle drink at a predictable time and place, revision of the herd becomes a virtually effortless task, usually performed from the cattleman's front porch (frequently from a hammock).

On the East Cape, around the villages of Los Barriles and Buena Vista gringos have established their little corner of paradise and constructed residences ranging from the ridiculous to the sublime. Co-existing with the aforementioned gringos is a number of indigenous villagers who own an uncensored herd of cattle. These villagers could not muster more than five acres of land among them but posses between fifty and one hundred free ranging horned nuisances. Gringo financed fence building is a major industry hereabouts.

During the dry season (usually from May to the summer rains in July or August) fodder becomes scare. It would never occur to the cattle owners to purchase feed for the cattle except in absolute desperation. Bossy considers all objects encountered in her search for nourishment. Cardboard boxes, empty cement sacks, and plastic shopping bags are included in the *vaca's* diet along with any greenery. On one remembered occasion the tail of a fabric-covered airplane appeased Bossy's raging appetite. Dan Brown swears that a cow drank two gallons of used motor oil at his place in Spa Buena Vista.

Fidel Lucero was the proprietor of a small grocery store across Highway 1 from the gas station in Los Barriles. Fidel had a way of ignoring incoming customers while he kept his nose buried in comic books. One afternoon while engaged in reading a particularly absorbing *photonovela,* he sensed a presence entering the front door but refused to heed it. When he finally decided to honor his customer with his attention, he discovered that the intruder was a cow who had consumed about half of a box of bananas in his produce department.

Horses enjoy the same freedom as the bovines but serve another purpose in the BC ranching scheme. Rancho Capilla and Rancho Los Martires have been the property of the Geraldo family since Dominican times (their land title was signed by Benito Juarez). Around forty head of horses show at the watering trough around sundown. During this authors thirty plus years acquaintance with these families a Geraldo has never been seen on horseback. Horses are status symbols. The Spanish word *caballero* (horseman) translates to gentleman, nobleman, knight or one of high station.

The reign of terror perpetrated by La Pelona the cow at La Capilla will be retold around gringo campgrounds for many decades. *La Pelona* (the bald one) was polled or hornless, hence the name. This black and white evil genius could consume a peck of potatoes from a hanging basket in the blink of an eye. Perhaps it should be explained that La Capilla is a rather casual trailer park located on the beach some two kilometers south of Rancho Buena Vista. Innocent first timers at La Capilla would set up their rig, extend the awning and immediately hang baskets of goodies for La Pelona's consumption. La Pelona was astute enough to recognize these unindoctrinated pilgrims and lurked in the bushes awaiting her chance. Oranges, apples, dry cereals, bananas, cabbages, tamales and on one remembered occasion a very large salad complete with blue cheese dressing were devoured by this cloven hoofed hussy.

Complaints to the management of the park launched a maximum-effort mission to locate the owners of this devious creature. No one came forward. Solicitations to law enforcement agencies for assistance were balefully ignored.

"When you have the cow in captivity, we will make an effort to locate the owner."

La Pelona continued her gourmet diet while numerous and sundry ruses were employed to effect her capture. Bush popper cowboys were imported from Miraflores. La Pelona retreated to the dense bush and thumbed her nose at them.

An ingenious snare trap described by Frank Buck, in his epic "*Bring 'Em Back Alive*," was installed and baited with alfalfa to no avail. The bait was changed to cabbage with the same negative results. Wilma Smith (a devious hussy herself) baited the snare with a watermelon rind and presto chango, one captured cow.

A slight design flaw in the snare was noted immediately after La Pelona's captured. One end of the rope was secured to a truck wheel, which proved to be of inadequate weight. The trailer park manager added the weight of his body to the intended anchor and this resulted in a terrifying Nantucket sleigh ride across the dry lakebed behind La Capilla.

La Pelona's valiant escape attempt was brought to a screeching hault when she maneuvered between two mesquite trees. The truck wheel was firmly jammed between the mesquite trunks and the manager came to rest hanging from a branch some five feet above the ground

The brand inspector was summoned and La Pelona's owner was identified. A meeting was held and attended by La Pelona, La Pelona's owner, the brand inspector, the trailer park manager, the district attorney and the municipal court judge. It was agreed that La Pelona's owner owed damages to the trailer park but in due consideration for the owner's financial state, damages would be waived if La Pelona was converted to hamburger and the trailer park manager received one kilogram of that hamburger. The hamburger was delicious. I know because I was that trailer park manager.

ABOUT RATTLESNAKES

*All natives of Baja California know this fact:

He who kills a rattlesnake on *Jueves Santo* (Thursday preceding Good Friday) is pardoned one hundred *amos* of purgatory. Doña Lupe assures us that an *amo* is an infinite amount, therefore, ten infinite amounts are something in the region of the national debt.

Rattlesnakes are aware of this fact. Hence, they keep a very low profile on *Jueves Santo* and chances of locating these critters on that special day are very slim, indeed.

René Cortez relates that the rattlesnake must meet his demise while he (the rattlesnake) is in good spirits. Since rattlesnakes seem to have a very short fuse, it would seem that total surprise would be a necessary element here.

Caminante (Traveler), Alex Flores's dog at Punta Colorada, killed a rattlesnake on *Jueves Santo* several years ago but since Caminante was not Catholic and most assuredly the rattlesnake was pissed, all bets were off, in the local concept.

On the morning of April 2, 1996, Tuesday, two days before *Jueves Santo*, Doña Lupe announced, rather hysterically, that a rattlesnake had invaded her canary's cage during the night and enjoyed a late supper. Investigation revealed the rattlesnake had sealed his doom as his girth was somewhat expanded by the canary within and he was unable to pass through the bars of the cage thus barring his escape. He was sleeping it off.

The cage containing snake et al was securely packaged and put away until Jueves Santo when justice was served and coincidentally a goodly amount of *amos* were deposited in the bank of purgatory. Might as well cover all bases.

ROSAS MARQUEZ

Corral Falso (False Corral), so named because of a natural rock formation that appears to be a man made rock corral, is located up a canyon about six miles west and about eighteen-hundred feet above Rancho Buena Vista. This is the home of the Rosas family. Something in the order of seventy-five souls live here, none more distant in relation than cousins.

About the only concessions to the twentieth century are concrete blocks instead of adobe, a few Japanese radios, some plastic kitchen utensils and a few old beat up trucks. Otherwise, not much has changed in the last century and a half. They still illuminate their homes with kerosene lamps and candles. This is curious since the Rosas Marquez clan (seven brothers) are the most esteemed *albañils* (masons) around the East Cape. Lupe, Evaristo (Shorty), Eliverto, Rafael, Francisco, Antonio, and Reginaldo travel down the steeply inclined rustic road from their home to Buena Vista and Los Barriles daily to erect some of the finest modern edifices in the area.

The Rosas brothers, as anyone in the area will testify, do beautiful work in stone, cinder block, tile, and plaster. Their homes at Corral Falso, conversely, are simple non-plastered concrete block structures, many with dirt floors, all with palm-thatched roofs and some without glass windows. Visiting gringos conclude that these humble dwellings are a product of poverty. This is untrue as the Rosas Marquez are some of the best paid artisans in the area and are owners of a sizable herd of cattle. It's really easy to explain. Hell, they have always lived that way and see no need for change. When they return each night, they escape the hustle and bustle of 2000 and return to 1850.

The Rosas brothers, except for very small jobs, work as a unit. There seems to be no boss in the pecking order as they each perform their assigned job in tranquil harmony with a constant banter (usually making Antonio or Francisco the goat) thus instilling a party atmosphere to the work-site.

The Rosas brothers are big strong men but six- foot -three-inch, two-hundred-forty pound Shorty, is the undisputed champ and a very gentle man. His robust good humor endears him to all.

The Rosas brothers refuse to become wage slaves. They

much prefer piecework as this, in their concept, gives them the dignity of contractors rather than common laborers. As contractors they reserve the privilege of working at their own pace. They are not encumbered with the puritan work ethic and while they are some of the most productive masons hereabouts they sometimes decide they have more pressing business elsewhere during the workday.

Shorty and Antonio were constructing a small *bodega* (warehouse) at Mini Super Playas del Tesoro last summer when a Corral Falso truck arrived in great haste. With no explanation other than "Doña Lupe, were leavin'!" they boarded the truck in a cloud of dust. Their departure caused no particular concern until investigation revealed they had left a half wheelbarrow of wet mortar and had not cleaned their tools.

The remaining five brothers were on another job nearby and had also departed summarily without explanation.

By noon the following day, none of the Rosas brothers had appeared. Doña Lupe was beside herself with worry and yours truly was dispatched to Corral Falso. It seems that one of Don Saturnino Rosas' little daughters had set fire to the house. Don Saturnino rescued his Winchester carbine from the flaming structure at the cost of rather severely burning his arms and had been transported to the hospital in La Paz.

The seven Rosas *albañils* begged our indulgence and promised to return to their jobs when Don Saturnino's house had been rebuilt.

Word of the fire was spread by the East Cape radio network and Mini Super Playas del Tesoro became a collection point for relief goods. When this writer arrived at the scene in a loaded pickup truck, Chacha Van Wormer and Silvia Eperline were already on site and off loading food, bedding, cooking utensils, dishes, silverware and even furniture.

Nine days elapsed before the Rosas brothers returned to their jobs on the beach. While involved in the reconstruction, they had decided that Don Saturnino's house was a bit cramped and should be expanded.

Corral Falso would be a good place to live me 'tinks.

MEXICO HIGHWAY 1

Some twenty-seven summers have come and gone since the inauguration of the trans-peninsular highway (Mexico Highway 1). During the time the road has existed a tradition seems to have developed that demands that anyone who sets out to publish some remarks on Baja California is compelled to include a dissertation on the effects of the road. The pre-road element is compelled to lament the existence of that damned asphalt ribbon laden with "Dina" trucks and "Winnebegos". The post-road element complains of the lack of shoulders and unavailability of gasoline for their "Winnebegos", and so it goes.

In the days of yore, the lack of a paved road was regarded by most of the pre-road gringos as a grand and glorious filter that kept the undesirables (in their thinking) out of the "real Baja". The southern limit of the trailer park crowd was somewhere around Colonia Colonet. Those wishing to venture further south were compelled to use specialized vehicles. Four-wheel-drive cars and trucks were popular, as was a smattering of motorcycles. Another group utilized private airplanes but these people confined themselves to the resorts and larger cities (mostly Loreto, Mulegé and La Paz) and had very little to do with the outback of Baja California.

The road has admittedly increased tourist traffic (BC's economic mainstay) a hundred fold during the past twenty-seven years and is therefore more than justified without considering the convenience it has created for the indigenous population.

Good ole buddy, Dave Deal, and yours truly were pondering these changes somewhere down the peninsula one evening and decided, since we had used mules, DC 10's, and all possible variables of conveyance in between, perhaps we were qualified to conduct some research to answer the question, "Has the road spoiled Baja California?"

We equipped ourselves with an array of scientific instruments including an open Jeep, a case of empty Tecate beer cans, three gallons of water and finally a one hundred-meter measuring tape. All possible variables were investigated and it was discovered that 6 1/4 ounces of water in a

Tecate beer can flung at a high trajectory from a Jeep moving fifty-seven miles an hour would come to rest thirty-one and a half meters from the center stripe of Mexico Highway 1. This optimum result was achieved on a still day with an ambient temperature of eighty-one degrees Fahrenheit

We therefore concluded that a trans-peninsular strip approximately sixty-three meters wide has been somewhat marred by Mexico Highway 1. Aside from this strip, Baja California is still out there for those who choose to search for it.

DRAWING BY DAVE DEAL

SANDBAGGED

Many backcountry ranchers here in southern Baja California possess historical artifacts ranging from pre-Hispanic arrowheads to objects from the Jesuit Mission period. These relics rightfully belong in a museum. Possession of the objects is unlawful. INAH (National Institute of Anthropology and History) serves as an enforcement agency in this matter and has power to confiscate these treasures and prosecute violators should they deem fit. Some of these objects have been in the hands of the old land grant families for centuries and are considered heirlooms. The ranch people are most reluctant to display their artifacts to a stranger since they fear confiscation and prosecution. However, they believe the objects have a cash value and will sometimes display them to a gringo who has approached them with the right attitude. This operation requires several visits to the same ranch to gain confidence of the rancher's family and prove that the gringo is not a treasure hunter. This writer spends considerable time and gasoline in high country locating these objects and trying to persuade the holders to donate them to the INAH Museum. Production has been slim to date.

Manuel de Ocio established Baja California's first silver mine at Santa Ana in 1748. This mine and the mill were active for a number of years. Ruins of this operation are yet present. Your reporter spends considerable time kicking around in the weeds up there and is on first name basis with many of the local people.

Enter Mario: Mario dropped by my digs a couple of months ago and casually mentioned that he had unearthed a silver chalice (possibly from a Jesuit altar) while hunting rabbits on the mesa above the old Ocio smelter.

"Some day, I'll bring it down to show you," he said on parting.

"You won't believe this!" he reported on our next meeting, "My oldest boy tried to clean that cup with a file. I'm afraid it has been damaged some but I'll bring it down one of these days." Mario tapped me for three hundred pesos before he departed.

Last week, he came equipped with the chalice. It was a lovely little thing. Negotiations were initiated and while waiting for Mario to spring the trap (price?), I inspected the object. Minute scrutiny under magnification revealed the words WEST COAST dimly engraved on the side of the loving cup. The subsequent engravings had been erased by file marks. As Mario was mentioning a price, I was overwhelmed by spasms of laughter.

You have to admire the guy! He must have done infinite research and planning to set this scam up, not to mention his time spent in pawnshops locating this "relic". His orchestration was superb. If there exists a hall of fame for great con artists, Mario certainly deserves a prominent monument.

TIMBABICHI

Arnold Senterfitt, in his book *Airports of Baja California*, described Rancho Timbabichi as being "just about as remote a place as you will find anywhere on earth." Timbabichi, located some seventy air miles south of Loreto on the western shore of the Mar de Cortes, has three possible modes of access: 1) by boat 2) by a twelve-mile mule ride from the nearest automobile road or 3) by air (oddly enough, there is a fairly serviceable airstrip of some seventeen-hundred feet in length there). The two families that live there, both named de la Toba, are supported by fishing, cheese making and a bit of cattle ranching.

The most striking feature of Rancho Timbabichi is the ruins of an old two-story adobe house off the north side of the runway. Atop this house, which was allegedly built as a vast pearling operation about a century past, grows a stately cardon cactus.

Something in the neighborhood of thirty years ago your reporter was blundering southbound in an old Cessna with some spare time and decided that a photograph of the cardon on top of the old ruin might come in handy for some future publication.

I had just landed when a rather stout matron approached the aircraft in startling haste and screamed, "God sent you, señor. God sent you!!"

"Just what is it that God has sent me for, señora?" I asked.

"We have a gravely ill *muchacha* here. She must see a doctor immediately."

La Paz has better medical facilities than Loreto and my intended destination was La Paz, so I advised the señora to load her daughter into the airplane and we should be able to contact a physician in less than an hour.

In about twenty minutes we were airborne with the patient, a pretty teenage girl, and her mother. The La Paz tower responded to our radio call and an ambulance was standing by when we landed. Mother and daughter were transported to Salvatierra Hospital while I remained at the airport to handle the paperwork with flight operations.

The patient was in recovery after surgery for an acute appendicitis when I arrived at the hospital.

After wandering around East Cape for about four days, I returned to Salvatierra Hospital to offer Señorita de la Toba a flight back to Rancho Timbabichi. However, my young friend had already been released and returned home.

Several months elapsed before I returned to Rancho Timbabichi and found Señorita de la Toba fat and sassy. "Now that you are well, would you like a pleasure ride in the airplane?" I offered.

She replied, "You don't believe I would ride in that damned thing if I weren't dying, do you?"

PANCHO VILLA, THE PROBLEM SOLVER

Dinner was finished at Rancho Agua Caliente. Ted Bonney and General Agustine Olachea sat on the veranda with brandy snifters in hand, watching a full moon rise over the Sea if Cortez. A long association had taught Ted that the old man's fondest memories were his experiences during the Mexican Revolution.

Ted baited the general into another story. "They tell me that during the revolution, you were a mean son-of-a-bitch."

"No, Teadoro, I was stern but not mean. Seems to me that you have been listening to my dog robber. Let me tell you a story of a mean son-of-a-bitch.

"I think it was the spring of 1915. I was an adjunct to the supreme commander in Mexico. My responsibility was Inspector General and entailed going into the field and reporting on the activities of the various commanders. I was dispatched to Hermosillo, Sonora, to prepare a report on the activities of General Francisco Villa. When I arrived in Hermosillo, I was very well received. When General Villa learned of my mission, he was pleased.

"'You come at a good time, General Olachea,' he said. 'We have a problem with a certain Colonel Vargas who commands a battalion in the highland to the east. Various citizens have come here to complain that there is practically no activity in his sector and the troops are loafing around town, drinking, carousing, molesting the women and eating up all the livestock. I would be most grateful if you would accompany me up there to resolve this problem.'

"We rode on horseback for two and a half days into the Sierra Madre. When we arrived at the Headquarters of Col. Vargas, we discovered he had learned of our coming and a fiesta to celebrate our arrival was in progress. We had lunch, watched cock fights and horse races in the afternoon, then retired for a siesta. After our siesta, dinner and dancing ensued and around midnight we finally departed to Col. Vargas' residence to discuss the purpose of our visit.

"'Colonel Vargas', Pancho Villa stated, 'reports have reached me that your troops have not ventured afield. It is alleged that your soldiers have become fat, lazy, drunk and women chasers. I would like an explanation.'

"Colonel Vargas reported, 'General Villa, in part, what you have heard is true. I have a very delicate situation here. Some three months ago I took a 19-year-old bride. I harbor the fear that if I should go into the field, and leave her alone my Lupita will become lonely and put the horns on me.'

"Pancho Villa pondered this for a short time and yelled into the kitchen, 'Señora Lupita could you step out here for a moment?'

"When Col. Vargas' bride came into the parlor, Pancho Villa regarded her solemnly for a moment, pulled his pistol and shot her four times. He turned to Col. Vargas and said, 'Now, Colonel, you don't have that problem any more. I suggest we get on with the war!'"

General Olachea sipped his brandy. "Now there, Ted," he said, "was a mean son-of-a-bitch."

As my memory serves me, this is exactly as the story was related to me by the late Ted Bonney.

FLYING TIGERS

Generalísimo Chiang Kai-shek was losing the war. The Japanese, with their state of the art air force, were bombing at their leisure since air defense in China was totally non-existent. Chiang recognized a need for expertise and consulted the US Embassy. The problem was ultimately passed down to the Air Attaché, Colonel Harvey Kenneth Greenlaw, a West Point graduate and military pilot. Harvey Greenlaw was summarily dispatched to the US to effect the purchase of a contingent of fighter airplanes.

The factors that motivated Harvey Greenlaw to select the Curtis P-40 are left to conjecture. Some say that he was able to work the best deal with Curtis while others maintain the P-40 Warhawk was actually the better aircraft for the job. After the airplanes were delivered, it was discovered that Col. Greenlaw had received a rather handsome commission on the sale. Whether this commission was paid by Chiang (Chinese business is still a mystery to the Western mind) or Curtis is still in question. Chiang would probably assume that a commission was due. The end result was that Col. Greenlaw was court-martialed and drummed out of the corps.

Chiang soon learned that his people could not possibly operate his new air defense system without a lengthy training period so he urgently searched for means by which to accomplish this instruction. He made H.K. Greenlaw commander of the new fighter force and once again Greenlaw was dispatched to the land of the Big PX to recruit experienced fighter pilots. His first selection was his old pal from his Randolph Field instructing days, Claire Chennault. Chennault was practically deaf as a result of many hours flying large radial engines and had been pensioned off by the Army. China was paying five hundred dollars a month and five hundred dollars a-kill, a fortune in those days. The American Volunteer Group to China was soon formed. Many of these pilots resigned commissions in the US Military to accept the job.

Madam Chiang was charmed by Chennault since she had learned English in a Georgia finishing school and

Chennault was from Louisiana. Over and above this, he played a formidable hand of bridge. In a short time, Chennault had aced old Harvey out and became the commander of the American Volunteer Group, demoting Harvey to operations officer. Chennault spent his days in the palace, while Harvey ran the Air Force.

After a few months of very effective operations three AVG pilots returned to the US (They said they resigned because of Greenlaw's tyranny, he said they were fired for insubordination). They put themselves in the hands of Hollywood screenwriters who re-named the AVG *The Flying Tigers* and re-wrote history. The resulting movie is now considered gospel on the subject.

The AVG was re-organized as the 14th Air Force when the US entered the war and all personnel were transferred in grade. Marine Corps and Navy pilots were allowed to return to their units if they so chose. Claire Chennault was appointed as Commanding General to this unit. Harvey K. Greenlaw had left the service in disgrace and therefore, was not accepted.

Greenlaw returned to the US, purchased a Duesenberg Roadster, checked into the Beverly Hills Hotel and invested heavily in a cartoon production company in Hollywood.

Cartoon production companies were involved in making training films for the military. Harvey's company was "frozen out" by military procurement officers and the company was soon broke.

In the spring of 1954 Harvey was residing in a little adobe and thatch *jacal* in El Arco, Baja California. He and Doctor Carlos McKinnon, along with some unnamed American associates, were making an effort to re-open the old Harding gold mine there. Doc McKinnon, a dentist, was a Scots/Australian emigrant to Baja who had lived on the peninsula some forty years. Doc and one of the investors flew to the mine by private airplane for an inspection tour. During this tour, Doc lamented that practically every ranch, road fork, hill, arroyo, and rock in Baja California had been named but nothing had been christened in his honor. He felt he had been slighted when one considered his tenure and stature in the community.

The morning subsequent to the inspection party's departure Harvey gave Juan Lopez and his sons the task of constructing an adobe *escusado* (privy) on a small hillock near his house. When the structure was completed, he affixed a sign proclaiming, SIERRA MCKINNON. He dispatched a telegram to Santa Rosalía as follows:

MCKINNON
BE ADVISED THAT A VAST MOUNTAIN HERE HAS BEEN CHRISTENED IN YOUR NAME - STOP
AN APPROPRIATE MONUMENT HAS BEEN CONSTRUCTED THEREUPON - STOP
I GO THERE EACH MORNING TO PAY HOMAGE - STOP
GREENLAW

Harvey chased mining scheme rainbows around Mexico for many years. He died in the early 1970's while trying to develop an opal mine near Compostella, Nayarit. The remains of this American hero lie in a pauper's grave in Compostella's *camposanto*, disregarded by history and forgotten by an ungrateful nation.

This writer was a guest in the Greenlaw digs in El Arco in April of 1954. During my stay the Colonel stated: "I suppose that, like everyone else, you'll write a book about this goddamn place after one trip down the peninsula."

I promised the Colonel that I had no intention of writing a book until I was qualified. I apologize to Colonel Greenlaw for breaking this promise but dammnit, I'm getting old and it's now or never.

FERNANDO

Preventative maintenance, in the Mexican concept, is abhorrent in the divine scheme. If it ain't broke, don't fix it. Automotive batteries and the related cables and connecting terminals demand a certain amount of attention in practically all environments, but it seems that machines working in the proximity of the beach are more prone to malfunction. A brief inspection will reveal impending problems with electrical components and this can be dealt with before complete failure occurs, but this is not the Mexican way. I repeat, "If it ain't broke, don't fix it." When an attempt to start an engine results in a resounding click from the solenoid, the first reaction is to grab some handy hard object (usually a rock) and pound the hell out of the offending terminal. If this system fails, then jumper cables and another battery are brought into play and the engine becomes operational. The problem has not been rectified.

I sauntered out of the repair shop at Rancho Buena Vista in the waning hour of a lovely April morning in a mellow mood to discover Fernando assaulting the battery terminals on an old AC Hd/5 tractor with a rock. He also made some very disparaging remarks about the aforesaid tractor's ancestry as two great gobs of green goop concealed the offending terminals.

"Fernando," says I, "let's thee and me do a bit of schoolhousin' on the care and feeding of battery terminals."

"You're the boss," he replied.

The battery posts were scrubbed with a wire brush. The negative cable was replaced, as was the cinch bolt on the positive cable. After re-assembly, an anti-corrosive spray was applied liberally. Electrolyte levels were brought to specification and the battery was charged for about half an hour.

"Okay, Fernando, try it now."

The Hd/5 responded with a cloud of black smoke and stabilized into a throaty rumbling idle.

"Learn anything, Fernando?"

"Sure did, boss, thanks for showing me."

"Not at all, buddy. Let's break for lunch."

Fernando walked about fifty feet to his old Pontiac and

hit the starter.

"KLICK, KLICK," it responded.

He popped the hood, dismounted, grabbed a handy rock and lambasted the terminals several times, remounted, started the car and complacently drove away.

Several weeks subsequent to these events, a solicitation for a character reference came across my desk. Seems Fernando wanted to become a policeman. My endorsement stated that in my opinion Fernando would make an outstanding policeman.

I was proven correct.

TRUQUEROS

A very special breed of men known as "truqueros del camino" plied their trade on the Camino Real prior to the inauguration of the Mexico Highway 1 in 1973. Ensenada, Santa Rosalía, Bahía Tortugas and La Paz were seaports and a goodly amount of merchandise was received by ship. Mulegé, Loreto, San José and San Lucas had occasional ship arrivals, but the volume of commerce into those ports did not justify regular maritime service. The truqueros handled most of the movement of goods.

Regular automotive traffic on the Camino Real was inaugurated around 1930 by a mail contract awarded to the Parra brothers, Raul, Luis and Juan. The Parra brothers operated their *diligencias* (stagecoaches) between Tijuana and Santa Rosalía. Gustavo Appel and an individual remembered only as "Chapo" handled the stagecoach route between Santa Rosalía and La Paz. Since mail and paying passengers were the primary concern, open touring cars (preferably Cadillac and Packard, circa 1928-1932) were used for these *diligencias*. These cars could be had for a song in the US during the depression and featured legendary ground clearance as well as five speed transmissions.

Diligencias carried around eight passengers, camping gear, bedding and mail sacks. A week was considered good time for a passage from Tijuana to Santa Rosalía.

Roadside ranches were way stations and served meals to passengers however, lunches were carried in case of breakdowns. *Mochilas* (bedrolls) were carried for all. Shelter but not bedding was furnished to women and children at the way stations. *Machos* were obliged to shift for themselves usually sleeping on the ground under the car.

Mechanical breakdowns, getting stuck in the sand (or mud) and flat tires were frequent occurrences. Winter rains played havoc with the road and certain sections became impassable. All hands were obligated to help with problems.

Tires and gasoline were unavailable with the advent of World War II; hence the *diligencias* became history.

A demand for shark liver as a vitamin supplement developed in the US about the time WW II came to a close.

RANCHO

Profits previously garnered by trucking freight to the south and returning to the north empty had not been substantial enough to create a regular truck route. Now however, northbound shark liver would be a motivating factor for trucks while the movement of foodstuff and hardware were deemed a back haul for the south. When chemical substitutes replaced shark liver in vitamins around 1953, commercial shark fishing on the Peninsula came to a sudden halt. While cattle, goats and a limited amount of seafood replaced shark liver north bound, it was not as lucrative and many of the *truqueros* dropped out. The hard core survivors became the "*truqueros del camino*" who literally lived on the Camino Real.

Trucks became the homes as well as the livelihood for these very rugged individuals. *Parillas* (storage racks) were fabricated above the truck cabs. *Parillas* were used for storage of the *mochila*, spare tires and tool kit. Grub boxes and storage for cooking utensils were hung beneath the cargo platforms (oddly enough, this identical arrangement is used by the Bedouin trucks in the deserts of Saudi Arabia, Kuwait and Jordan). Dual wheels were not used, as the road was too narrow. Rocks outside the narrow road caused much damage to the tires. A single centered rim designed to follow the same track as the front wheels was used and 11"x 20" wheels were installed in the rear. Heavy-duty springs and an electric two-speed rear axle were standard. Normal loads were around seven tons on a truck designed for two-and-a-half tons.

The *Baja Californios* held these knights of the road in high esteem and most boys aspired to be *truqueros* when they grew up.

The trail had it's own stern code (apologies to Robert W. Service). No motorist was ever left stranded. A *truquero* might loose days assisting a stalled vehicle but no payment was expected or received.

Some of the adventures of the *truqueros* are retold in villages and ranchos today. Mayo and Tavo Villavicencio along with Hector Montoya were northbound, loaded with cattle, when a deluge trapped them at El Socorro. They remained mired there for seven weeks. The cattle were off loaded and turned out to graze. Not only were seven calves born during the stay at El Socorro but also the pasturage there was outstanding, adding weight to the cattle for market.

Alberto Ojeda's world was the forty-eight miles lying between San Ignacio and Santa Rosalía. He drove trucks for Manuel Meza for thirty-one years on the same route. Loaded, about five hours were required to traverse one leg of the route, assuming that nothing went amiss. Alberto was responsible for all maintenance and repair on his trucks as well as completing an average of eighteen round trips a month. He spent very little time at his home in San Ignacio. Four trucks were expended during that thirty-one years of traversing some of the roughest terrain on the Camino Real. After 6,696 round trips, Don Alberto had an intimate acquaintance with this section of the Camino Real.

Highway I brought an end to the *truqueros* but their legend continues to live in the hearts of the people of present day Baja.

WHAT I'M SAYING IS NOT WHAT YOU ARE HEARING

The Baja California Mexican abhors specifics. When asked about distance, "How far to La Paz?" He answers, "An hour and a half." This is quite remarkable since there is a road sign at each kilometer advising the distance.

He approaches a grocery clerk and announces, "I want a pack of cigarettes."

"What kind of cigarettes?"

"The same as I bought last week."

"I don't recall selling you cigarettes last week."

"They were Marlboros."

"Lights or regulars?"

"The cigarettes in the red pack."

The clerk produces the Marlboro regulars in the red pack and states, "Ten pesos, please."

Our hero replies, "But these are in a box. I want those in a soft pack!"

He never says, "I missed my bus." He reports, "My bus left me!"

He never says something is lost or misplaced. It is *guardado* ("put away") but he can never remember where it is *guardado*.

He never makes a definite appointment. "I'll see you Tuesday," you say.

"If God wills it," he replies. This puts the horse on God. If he doesn't show, it was God's fault. He will show two weeks late for an appointment and never mention it.

"Ni modo." ("Fate has it.")

***

Mexico is the only place known where a hangover is a legitimate excuse for not appearing for work. Our hero works on his car on Saturday, gets drunk on Sunday and does not show for the job on Monday. They call this "*San Lunes*" (Saint Monday).

***

Mark Willis, an American resident in La Ribera, loaned a saw to a neighbor. After a year had passed, Mark went to the neighbor's house to reclaim his saw. The neighbor was outraged. "But I haven't finished using it," he said.

***

Mañana does not mean "tomorrow" as popularly supposed. *Mañana* means "not today" or "sometime in the future, God willing."

***

The slowest thing in the world is a Mexican funeral with only one set of jumper cables.

***

The most popular man at a Mexican wedding is the owner of the jumper cables.

***

The Baja California state flower is the discarded Tecate beer can.

***

Volkswagens are called *ombiligos* (navels) in Mexico because everybody has one.

***

Prior to the existence of the trans-peninsular highway people seldom left their villages. Social intercourse was restricted to a degree that some phrases and speech patterns were unique to a certain village or ranching area. While this is still true in very isolated areas it is dying out with more available sources of communication, especially radio and television. A person using the phrase "*sí pues malina*" ("you're shinning me on") was immediately recognized as being from San Ignacio. "*Vosotros*" (archaic Spanish for "you all") labeled the user as a resident of the Sierra San Francisco.

***

Many words were coined for unfamiliar objects or perhaps the user thought his word more descriptive:

gato	(cat)	automotive jack
topo	(gopher)	bulldozer
mapache	(raccoon)	starter motor on large tractors
araña	(spider)	rake
chicharra	(locust)	jackhammer
burros	(jackass)	carpenter's saw horse
caguama	(sea turtle)	quart of beer (also called a *ballina* [whale])
gusano	(worm)	six wheel drive truck
perras	(female dogs)	vice grips
perros	(male dogs)	load binders
pluma	(feather)	writing pen
tripa	(gut)	garden hose
perricos	(parrots)	sheet metal shears
esposas	(wives)	handcuffs

AIRPLANES

At the inception of the Baja California fishing resorts in the early 1950's, private aircraft were about the only transportation available because commercial air transport was inadequate and no road existed. Each resort had its own airstrip. Hanger flying got equal time with fishing stories at the cocktail hour. Astute fishing resort management did about as much advertising in aviation oriented publications as they did in those intended for the sport fisherman. A small airplane was considered an essential to resort operations, as a fishing boat. Those were the golden days. Airport personnel were mostly Baja California people (mainland officials march to the beat of another drummer) and had an easy rapport with frequently returning private pilots.

Private flying experienced a complete reversal in official attitudes with the coming of Mexico Highway I and statehood for the Peninsula. Officials had received tips on occasion from grateful pilots when service and courtesy merited. Ultimately the customary gratuity was demanded and took on the aspect of *mordida* (a bribe) resulting in friction between experienced BC fliers and airport officialdom. On several occasions, appeals to the Aircraft Owners and Pilots Association created boycotts until remedies were effected.

The US Customs and Immigration services seemed to have changed their attitude toward private aircraft traffic about the same time as the Mexicans, but for other reasons. Narcotics smuggling had been limited to the coast along the Gulf of Mexico until the Airborne Warning and Control System and other tools forced operations further west. Efforts to intercept these *narcótico traficantes* led to new regulations on both sides of the border. Arriving aircraft were required to report their impending arrival an hour in advance. Variables of fifteen minutes between estimated time of arrival and actual landing carried fines of around five hundred dollars with no recourse.

Elizabeth Dole became Secretary of Transportation and hence the director of the Federal Aviation Agency. Ms. Dole regarded private aircraft with a baleful eye indeed. In her concept any small airplane in flight was an encroachment on her god given airspace and had to be eliminated. She was very effective. Her underlings, previously esteemed as tolerant, amiable good ol' boys became junk yard dogs dressed in seersucker suits, white shoes and drove gray Plymouths bearing logos: "FOR OFFICIAL USE ONLY." They caught us with our pants down.

Liberal shysters seized the opportunity and the courts handed out unbelievable decisions with outlandish awards in lawsuits against light plane manufacturers. Piper, Cessna, and Beach were forced to suspend light aircraft manufacturing when the cost of liability insurance exceeded the cost of building the aircraft. This resulted in prohibitive prices on used aircraft as well.

Most of the old gang who romped around Baja's skies sold their airplanes. The dudes who are served up in DC 9's today aren't the same people we enjoyed in the days of yore. In the land of Willie Clinton and Rodney King they call this progress. Glad I don't live there any more.

YARNS OF SAN IGNACIO

The ecological balance in the valley of San Ignacio Kadakaaman is found in all the species there. When the saturation point of population is reached, the young usually seek a more habitable environment. Homo sapiens are not exempt from this law. The limited resources of the valley have forced the young males to pursue their fortunes in other locales, usually in the fish camps on the Pacific Coast. Since Mexican custom dictates that nice girls don't leave home until married, a glut of unmarried females has always existed in this pueblo.

Until about thirty years ago the pacific lobster and abalone camps were extremely primitive, with no medical facilities, no schools, no electricity, and fresh water was hauled in. Families stayed in San Ignacio while papa fished. At this writing the situation has changed slightly and the younger families live in the coastal pueblos.

In the days of yore, the lobster fishing season terminated on March fifteen and the men returned to San Ignacio ready for a rip-snorting fiesta. After a couple of weeks, finances began to dwindle and the pace slowed. The men sort of loafed around the plaza until fishing resumed in October. Travelers, unfamiliar with the situation, concluded that San Ignacio had the laziest men in the world.

It was reported that a city ordinance required tennis shoes on the burros so as not to disturb the sleeping loafers in the plaza. Another ordinance required that rooster's vocal cords be severed for the same reason. Composing yarns about the *huevons of* San Ignacio soon became one of Baja California's favorite pastimes.

San Ignacio's favorite daughter is national television comedian Yuyu Blengio. Yuyu knew a good thing when she saw it and put scriptwriters to work on the theme, resulting in national fame for the pueblo.

Pedro and Pancho are enjoying an afternoon *siesta* when Pancho opens one eye, "Would you look at that?"

"Look at what *compadre*?" Pedro doesn't open an eye.

"Well, the wind is blowing a ten peso bill down the street."

Minutes pass when Pancho says, "Do you think we should pick it up, *compadre*?"

"Naw, *compadre*, everyone hereabouts knows the wind changes around four o'clock. It'll come back."

***

Don Antonio has just finished his afternoon *siesta* and is relaxing in his favorite rocking chair on the patio with a cup of coffee. Doña Maria is patting *tortillas* in the kitchen.

"*Vieja* (old woman), do you remember the remedy your Aunt Matilde used for a rattlesnake bite?"

"Well, let me think about it," mused Doña Maria. "Seems to me that she boiled the bark of the *palo blanco* for a while, then she added the pith from the cordon cactus. After this had simmered a bit, she put in a bit of *chili* and some *canela*. There may have been some more ingredients, I'm not sure. Why do you ask? Did a rattlesnake bite you?"

"No," yawned Don Antonio. "It's just that one is coming up the garden path."

***

Mesquite is the preferred *lenya* (firewood) in Baja California. San Ignacio householders demand that this *lenya* is of uniform diameter and length. Centuries of harvesting mesquite has about depleted the supply in the proximity of the village, forcing the *lenyeros* (woodcutters) further into the canyons each year for quality firewood. *Lenyeros* take pack burros into the high country where they camp for several days to load their pack trains. Don Filomino enjoys the best reputation among the *lenyeros*. He returns from the sierra with more than half of his production consigned. The remaining firewood is sold on spec. Don Filomino can often be found reclining in the shade of the Indian Laurel trees that cover San Ignacio's plaza. He is surrounded by loaded burros thereby expediting immediate delivery when a buyer appears.

Our hero was thus engaged on a fine spring morning when a sewing machine salesman from Tijuana approached.

"*Señor Lenyero*, can you please tell me the time?"

Don Filomino leisurely extended his left hand to the south end of the nearest animal, hefted the burro's testicles a bit and replied, "*Señor*, it is half past ten."

The sewing machine salesman thanked the *lenyero* graciously and set off in an effort to vend sewing machines on time payment plans, but his heart just wasn't in it. His thoughts kept returning to the *lenyero* who could tell time by hoisting a burro's balls. He returned to Don Filomino's post and queried, "*Señor,* I'm sorry to be a bother, but could you tell me the hour?"

Don Filomino repeated his performance and replied, "It is now 11:17 am."

The sewing machine salesman mumbled his thanks and retired to the far side of the plaza to ponder the marvelous thing he had witnessed. Soon he could bear it no longer and returned to Don Filomino stating, "*Señor*, I will pay you fifty pesos to teach me your trick."

"What trick?" Don Filomino was puzzled.

"One hundred pesos?"

"Very well, but what trick?"

"The trick of knowing the hour by lifting a burros balls."

"Oh, that trick," exclaimed the canny *lenyero*. "To teach you to tell time by lifting the burros balls I will require prepayment."

The sewing machine salesman forked over one hundred pesos.

"First off," stated Don Filomino, "when one grasps the scrotum of a burro, it must be accomplished with a tender authority, or the burro will take offense and kick the hell out of the grasper: thusly." Don Filomino demonstrated. "Can you handle that?"

"I think so."

"Good, then let's exchange positions."

When the sewing machine salesman was comfortably seated leaning against the tree trunk, Don Filomino advised, "Remember, firmly but gently."

The sewing machine salesman timidly reached out and lifted the burro's gonads. The burro turned his head and stared balefully but made no other movement. The sewing machine salesman sweated profusely.

"Splendid, splendid," exclaimed the *lenyero*. "Now, if you will look under your hand, you will observe a clock in the window of Meza's Store across the street. That clock is never wrong!"

This piece was written in San Ignacio something over 30 years ago...

I'm not sure if it is poetry or the ravings of a lunatic:

SAN IGNACIO

Days ending in a spectacle of color behind palms...
Bougainvillea... hibiscus...grapes coming into foliage...
Orange blossoms... wind... dirt...
Dogs barking in the night....

Roosters crowing in the early morning...
Canvas cots... mescal... beer... billiards...
Lovely muchachas promenading in the plaza in the evenings....
Jukeboxes played at maximum volume in cantinas...

Pungent odors of frijoles and tortillas
Cooking over breakfast fires...dates... strong coffee....
Cuca Castro singing in the patio as she does a washing...
Niñas playing in the irrigation canal...
Domino games in Hercilia's store....

Cleopatra's pool where we swam... mail on Wednesday
And Saturday... badly maintained engines in old trucks
Protesting as they climb hills... badly toned mission bells
ringing at 6:00 A.M...
The little reed lined lake with the dam crossing its exact center...
Barbecued cow's heads at El Oasis Restaurant...

Daniel Romero's hideous purple house with yellow trim
Around the doors and windows...kerosene lamps...
Pack mules in the streets laden with firewood...
Delighted niños playing fully clothed in summer rain storms...
A palm log for sitting and drinking beer...

Tia Chala clucking at her chickens... delicious wine...
Leree's smelly escuzado... children reciting catechisms…
Chino Meza strolling restlessly in the plaza as he waits for a taxi fare…
The Moorish mission... ranchers shopping in Meza's General Store…

Berta Cota making her own wine, stomping out the purple…
Truck drivers sleeping in their clothes on the benches in the plaza, snoring louder than one could believe possible…
Baby goats gamboling on the rocks... Moni Romero kissing her novio on the door stoop, caught in the lights of a passing automobile…

Baby kittens wrestling under a fig tree... brassy days in July....
Windy days in January... Mariachis playing until 3:00 A.M....
Drunken fishermen yelling their exuberance... baby Chuey calling the Americans gringos…
Concha and Loloy sneaking a cigarette in Hercilia's patio…

San Ignacio…